Battle at Circle Four

Since time began the range had been open wild land, roamed first by buffalo, and then by cattle, herded by the ranchers to feed a growing nation. The railroad, too, had come, linking east to west and bringing cattle buyers.

But now a new force was moving in. A great mining company began to drive the ranchers off the range, taking the land for themselves. Their only law was that of the six-gun. Angry and frightened, ranchers began looking for someone to help them fight this new menace.

Bob Nevin broke out of jail when word came to him of what had been happening. The mining corporation had forced his father and his neighbours to the edge of bankruptcy. Determined to protect his family Nevin rode back to the valley, finding that it was one huge powder-keg and his arrival merely the fuse – ready to blast everything into violence . . . .

Doncaster
Metropolitan Borough Council

DONCASTER LIBRARY AND INFORMATION SERVICES

Please return/renew this item by the last date shown.
Thank you for using your library.

InPress 0231 May 06

3012202080891 7

Battle at Circle Four

Luke Holt

A Black Horse Western

ROBERT HALE · LONDON

© John Glasby 1966, 2003
First hardcover edition 2003
Originally published in paperback as
The Loner by Chuck Adams

ISBN 0 7090 7247 3

Robert Hale Limited
Clerkenwell House
Clerkenwell Green
London EC1R 0HT

Typeset by
Derek Doyle & Associates, Liverpool.
Printed and bound in Great Britain by
Antony Rowe Limited, Wiltshire

CHAPTER ONE

GUN HIGH

The stranger rode into Benson an hour this side of sundown and Sheriff Will Rowland put his appraisal on him the moment he spotted him on the black roan. He thought he had every type of man figured during the seven years he had been sheriff, but this man had him beat. There was something about him that he couldn't quite put a name to; a climbing tenseness which seemed to be focused on the man in a curiously indefinable way. He rode tall in the saddle like a man sure and confident of himself and let his keen-eyed gaze sweep along the deep-shadowed boardwalk, giving every man he saw a swift glance, watchful for trouble, a man to whom danger was nothing new.

Rowland rubbed a hand down the side of his face thoughtfully as he watched the other ride by heading in the direction of the livery stable. He had the feeling that all hell was going to break loose very soon and that he would be powerless to stop it. The only thing he had recognized about the other were the guns strapped low with their smoothly polished butts, evidence of long use; and that look about him which spoke, more plainly than words, that he was in town looking for somebody.

5

The rider moved around the corner of the street at the crossroads in the middle of the town, and Rowland, after hesitating for a moment, angled through the inch-deep dust of the street towards his office. Stopping on the board-walk, he swept the brim of his hat back, squinted up at the slowly-darkening sky, then went inside, humming a little tunelessly to himself, a sure sign that he was more than usually uneasy in his mind. Silently he cursed the whims that brought men into his town on these errands of vengeance and revenge, making life twice as difficult for him as it would normally be. Sinking down into the chair behind the desk, he placed his feet up, leaned back, built himself a smoke. The day had been hot with a scorching sun beating down cruelly on the town from a cloudless sky and even the coming of evening had brought little coolness to the air which fastened itself in a man's throat as though it had been drawn over some vast oven before reaching his lungs.

The sound of footsteps on the boardwalk outside reached him a moment later and the door opened to admit a tall, gangling, awkward-looking man in his late forties, the deputy's badge pinned on his shirt. He closed the door quietly behind him, walked into the room. He said indifferently: 'I figure we may have got ourselves some trouble tonight, Sheriff.'

'That *hombre* who rode into town a while ago?' Rowland's brows went up a little and he swung his legs to the dusty floor.

'That's right.' Bessard nodded. 'Don't recollect havin' seen him around these parts before, but he's sure got that look about him. I'd recognize it anyplace.'

'Ain't no point lookin' through the wanted posters I got. I'd know that face if I'd seen it before,' Rowland said stiffly. He got to his feet, hitched his gunbelt up a little around his middle. 'Reckon the best thing to do is find him and have a

6

little talk with him. If he's got the killin' fever, sooner I know about it, the better.'

'Want me to come along with you, Will?'

'No. I figure I can handle this.' Moving out on to the boardwalk, he searched for a cooling breeze, but found none. The street was all but deserted for this was supper time, a slack period in town. A darting lizard skittered through the dust, vanished into the gloom beneath the wooden slats of the opposite boardwalk. He said over his shoulder: 'I'll check with Ben at the livery stable first, then go on to the saloon. Guess those are the places he'll make for first.'

He paused for a moment outside the livery stable, then went in. It was cooler here than out on the street. The groom stepped out from the stalls at the back, bent a little now with advancing years, but his eyes still as clear as ever. Not much missed his gimlet gaze.

'That stranger ride in here a while ago on the black roan, Ben?' Rowland asked.

The other grinned slyly. 'Figured you might be along askin' about him, Will. Sure, he brought his mount in. It's back yonder in the end stall. You want to see it?'

'No.' Rowland shook his head. 'I'm more interested in the man than the bronc he was ridin'. '

'Queer critter. Didn't talk much,' observed the other. 'Sure looked a mean cuss with a gun though.'

'So you saw that too,' mused Rowland. 'You got any idea where he was headed after he left here?'

'The saloon. He was askin' about Charlie Duffield. You reckon he's got somethin' against Charlie?'

'Could be at that. Duffield is a bad customer, lightnin' fast with a gun. He's killed plenty of men along the cowtrail into Texas from what I've heard, and made plenty of enemies in the process. If this stranger has come ridin' in for a showdown with Duffield, then there'll sure be sparks aflyin' when those two meet.'

'Duffield usually gets into town around nine,' volunteered the other, 'with the rest of the Bar X crew.'

Rowland nodded, consulted his watch, then thrust it back into his pocket. 'Another hour or so yet. Guess I'd better have a word with this *hombre* myself before those boys from the Bar X get here. I don't want any trouble in town if I can stop it, even if I have to lock this fellow up until mornin'.'

He made his way to the Lonesome Trail saloon, a tight, worried look on his face. Some of the other citizens had seen the stranger ride in and there was a hanging stillness lying over everything now. Yellow light spilled from the batwing doors as he approached and early though it was, a couple of drunks staggered down the steps and moved unsteadily across the street.

It was too early in the evening for much business in the saloon and the customers were few, so it was easy to pick out the stranger standing by himself against the bar, resting his weight on his elbows. As Rowland put in an appearance, most of the talk in the saloon stopped, as though cut off with a knife and Will saw the man at the bar stiffen a little, but giving no other outward sign that he had spotted him in the mirror that ran the whole length of the saloon behind the bar.

The bartender glanced quickly as though appraising any trouble, then relaxed a little as he saw Rowland. The sheriff walked to the bar, stopped a couple of feet from the stranger, motioned with one finger to the barkeep and took his drink with his left hand, not once taking his glance off the man beside him. Very quietly, he said. 'I noticed you ride into town a little while ago, mister. Mind if I ask you why you're here?'

The other turned slowly. He had a coldly handsome face and the palest grey eyes that Rowland had ever seen. He

8

drained his glass in a leisurely fashion, set it down on the bar before replying. 'I'm lookin' for a man, Sheriff.' he said calmly. 'I've heard I might find him here.'

'And when you do find him – what happens then?'

The other shrugged his shoulders. 'I've got business with him. A lot is goin' to depend on what he does.'

It had been quiet in the saloon before that but suddenly it was deathly still. The man had spoken his words softly yet they seemed to have carried to every corner of the room. The card players at the nearby tables stopped their playing and eyed him watchfully, suspiciously.

'I'm not sure what you intend to do, but I reckon I'd better warn you that I want no trouble here in Benson. It's my job to see that law and order is kept and I mean to do that by any means I figure best. I ain't aimin' to see this saloon, or town, shot up and that's just where this kind of talk leads. I've seen it happen before. So I'm warnin' you, mister—'

'The name's Nevin, Sheriff. Bob Nevin.'

'Well, Nevin, I'm not just warning you, I'm tellin you. Stay clear of trouble, and that means gunplay. I've heard you've been askin' about Duffield. He's the top man with the Bar X outfit.' Rowland let his glance fall significantly towards the guns strapped low at the other's waist, noticing again the smooth handles worn by long use, then went on: 'Maybe you're faster with a gun than Duffield, although I doubt it. But if you've got an argument with him, and you do manage to kill him, it won't help you much. The whole Bar X outfit will be on your neck before you get a chance to ride clear of town. And even you couldn't buck that crew.'

'Thanks for the warnin' anyway, Sheriff.'

Rowland emitted a patient sigh. 'Just stay out of trouble while you're in town, that's all.'

The other reached out for the bottle, poured himself another glass and stared down at the amber liquid for a moment. Then he said evenly. 'I'm afraid that I can't oblige you there, Sheriff. This business I've got with Duffield. It's gone too far for that.'

Rowland pursed his lips tightly for a long moment. He knew now that his first impression of Nevin had been right after all. The other was no more than a killer on the loose, running along a vengence trail a mile wide and he wouldn't stop until he reached the end of it, no matter how many men died along the way.

It was at times like this that Rowland regretted the day he had accepted the post of sheriff in Benson. Trouble very rarely occurred, despite the breed of some of the men taken on by the various ranch crews. The gunslingers and owlhoots who rode in looking for work and a chance to stay one jump ahead of any trouble that lay on the trail behind them, found that so long as they stayed out of trouble in Benson, they were all right. By some unwritten, mutual agreement they settled any differences and personal feuds elsewhere, but this looked different.

'What you got against Duffield that makes you so allfired ready to shoot it out with him?' he asked. 'You some fast gun from way up north.'

'No, I'm a cowman. But a couple of friends of mine got killed a little while ago in Twin Forks and it was this coyote Duffield who killed them.'

'So now you're gunnin' for him.'

'What else can a man do? Seems there was law of a kind in Twin Forks, but no justice.' Without taking his eyes from Rowland, he went on thinly: 'Is it the same here? The big men givin' the orders?'

'It sure as damn ain't,' snapped the sheriff harshly. He suddenly had his fill of arguing. These last few minutes had triggered off his uncertain temper and he went on savagely: 'Now I'm givin' you fair warnin'. Any shootin' and I'll lock you in jail so fast you won't know what happened. That is, if

10

you're still on your feet after Duffield has finished with you.'

'I'll bear that in mind, Sheriff.' The other tossed back his drink, then turned away.

The other's blunt words grated on Rowland's taut nerves, but he held his temper in check. His searching gaze rested on the other's face for a moment, then he shrugged, turned and walked out of the saloon.

Nevin finished his drink, pushed his hat on to the back of his head and looked across at the bartender. The other noticed again that he used his left hand, his right never being very far from the gun at his hip.

'This sheriff you've got here,' he said his eyes fixed levelly on the other. 'What sort of a man is he?'

The bartender pulled the damp cloth from his belt and wiped it over the top of the bar for a moment, considering. 'You mean does he work in cahoots with any of the big ranchers in the territory?'

'Somethin' like that.'

'Well, he don't,' was the straight reply. 'And don't let that awkward look fool you. There's more'n one man figured Rowland was a pushover with a gun, only to end up in a pine box on Boot Hill. The Bar X crew rides into town now and again to let off steam, but they don't give any trouble.'

'And Duffield works for the Bar X?'

'He's the foreman. Mostly they're gunslingers and owlhoots, but Duffield did one thing for 'em. He made them into a crew and he's got some loyalty from them which means a lot.' His eyes narrowed a shade. 'Now you can see what Rowland meant when he said that if you killed Duffield, you'd have to buck the whole crew.'

Nevin straightened. 'You got any idea where I can get a bed for the night?'

The other jerked a thumb. 'There's the hotel along the street a piece. You can get a bed there.'

'Thanks.' Nevin tossed a couple of coins on to the bar,

11

made his way out of the saloon. He was, by habit, a quick-moving, restless man and he chafed at the slow passage of time since he had ridden into this town. He had the feeling that Duffield was very close, that he was near the end of the trail which he had followed so diligently for several weeks.

Jeb Caldwell and Joe Fordham had been born and raised with him in a small cow town in Northern Montana, had ridden together, punched cows on the range that covered most of the territory and taken one of the big herds through to Abilene along the Chisholm Trail. Then the other two had moved on and the last he had heard, they had bought a small place and started their own beef herd.

He had lost track of them for close on two years and then, from a chance remark in a saloon, had discovered that there had been a shoot-out in the town, that both Jeb and Joe had been shot down by a man named Duffield. Neither of them had been a gunman and whether the story that they had drawn first was true or not, it had certainly not been a fair fight. And Duffield had been allowed to get off free, set loose by the crooked sheriff who ran the town of Twin Forks.

He found himself wondering now, as he made his way towards the hotel, the only two-storied building along that stretch of the main street, whether things might not have been different if he had only decided to stay with them, maybe thrown in his lot on the ranch they had hoped to build up together. Maybe if he had been around at that time, he could have saved both of his friends from Duffield's gun. But the trouble had been that he had been governed by that restless, footloose habit which had seized the three of them in the early days, and he had not been back home for almost five years now, back to that green valley between the Snowy Hills. He was headed there now, but first he had this chore to take care of.

He trailed his spurs through the dust, climbed up on to

the hollow-echoing boardwalk outside the hotel, pushed open the doors with the flat of his hand and stepped inside. There was a sleepy-eyed clerk behind the desk. He sat up more straight on his chair as Nevin stepped up to the counter, found himself staring into a pair of steel-grey eyes which held his own, sending a little shiver of nameless apprehension through him.

'You got a room I can have for the night?' Nevin asked.

The other nodded, swallowed visibly. He turned the register, handed the other the pen.

'Sure thing, mister. Upstairs, third on the right. You figure on havin' a bath? I can get the swamper to draw hot water for you. Two bits extra.'

'Sure. Call me when it's ready.'

He saw the other glance down curiously at the name in the register as he took his key and started for the stairs, though he knew that the name would mean nothing to the clerk. The stairs creaked underfoot and there was the smell of dust in his nostrils as he reached the top, found his room and opened the door, going inside and locking it after him.

Unbuckling his gunbelt, he placed it over the corner of the chair near the bed, then went over to the window and stood for a moment looking down into the quiet street. It seemed a quiet town on the surface, yet in spite of this, there was a deep undercurrent, a climbing tenseness which he had noticed the minute he had ridden in. Whether it was something focused on him, or whether it had been there before he had arrived was something he did not know. A couple of men walked across the street to the saloon. A shaft of yellow light fell on to the grey dust as they went inside, was then blotted out as the doors swung shut. A solitary rider paced slowly down the centre of the street and as he passed the window, Bob saw him glance up, caught the glimmer of light on the sheriff's star he wore on his shirt. Evidently Rowland was taking his job of watching the town seriously. He felt inwardly that the lawman was a straight and honest man, trying to do his job fairly and as well as he could, unlike that snake in Twin Forks who merely carried out orders handed down to him by the powerful ranchers. It was a thankless and often dangerous job that straight-shooting sheriffs did in frontier towns such as this and he did not envy Rowland his task, was faintly sorry that he might have to be the one to make it even more difficult.

There was a brief knock on the door and the clerk's voice called: 'Bath's ready for you any time you want it, Mister Nevin.'

'Thanks, I'll be right out.' He went out, locking his door behind him, followed the other down to the small side room where a tin bath full of steaming water stood waiting for him. He lazed luxuriously in it, letting the weariness and the tenseness soak out of his limbs. It felt good after these long, hard days on the trail and he relaxed in it until the water began to grow cold. Towelling himself briskly, he put on his clothes again, feeling some of the life back in his body.

Cruising into the small dining room, he sat down and ordered supper, making himself a smoke before it arrived. There were few other guests there and most of the other tables were empty. The food, when it came, was well cooked and he ate ravenously, sitting back and letting all of his muscles fall loose, enjoying the laziness which came after the long trail he had followed, the long days in the blister-ing heat of the sun and the cold, chill camps he had made, out on the desert or in the high hills.

When he had finished, he washed the dinner down with hot black coffee, found that while he had been weary earlier, the supper and coffee had acted as a stimulant and he felt warm and alive. The chill restlessness came back into his mind as he at there, turning past events over in his brain.

Going back up to his room, he stood next to the window, pressing himself back against the wall so that he could not be seen from below. He did not bother to light the lamp, but stood in the darkness, eyeing everyone in the street. He had been standing there for less than five m:nutes when a man yelled loud and long somewhere at the far end of the street and a moment later, a gun sounded, the shot echoing up and down the street. There were more gunshots, the sound of running horses.

Nevin watched closely, saw the tightly-bunched group of riders bearing down on the saloon across the way, reining up their mounts in front of it, dismounting on the run, thrusting their guns back into their holsters before piling in through the batwing doors. He forced himself to relax although the tightness was still growing in his mind. That was obviously the Bar X crew letting off their high spirits. If he was right, then Duffield would be down with them. For a second, the idea of bracing the whole crew so long as he got Duffield first came into his mind, but he dismissed it at once. Rashness would be fatal in circumstances such as this. Caution was the quality he would need. He recognized that the old ways of violence, never different, never changing, could work their way with the swiftness of a prairie fire through this small frontier town once he called Duffield.

Taking his gunbelt from the chair, he buckled it on, checked the guns in their holsters, then walked to the door, went out and made his way down the creaking stairs, through the small lobby and into the street. The group from the Bar X had gone into the saloon now and he could hear their raucous yelling as they began their night's drinking. He hesitated for a moment, then returned to the livery stable to water his horse, walked idly back and stood in the cool stream of air that blew down one of the narrow alleys at the side of the stables.

He paused there and then turned to walk back to the saloon when the quiet voice came to him out of the darkness.

'You waitin' for Charlie Duffield, stranger?'

'That's right.' Nevin spoke without turning. The groom came out of the dimness and stood beside him. He had a sly humour on his wrinkled features and his eyes were bright-sharp like those of a magpie.

'He didn't ride in with that bunch,' observed the other. A pause, then: 'You got the makings of a smoke on you?'

'Sure.' Bob handed over his pouch. He guessed that this man saw and heard more than most of what went on in the town, that he might be useful. 'You know where he is?'

'Maybe I do and maybe I don't.'

'Meanin' you don't intend to say?'

'I didn't say that. But you seem to be in too much of an all-fired hurry. If you act like this when you're facin' Duffield, you'll be stretched out in the dust before you know where you are and' – he added softly, slyly – 'with a bullet in your back.'

'How'd you figure that?'

'Charlie never takes chances, that's why he's lasted so long. Sure, he'll meet a man in fair fight, just so long as he knows for certain that the other ain't no gunman and he can take him with one hand strapped behind his back. But if he ain't sure, or if he knows that he's up against a hardened case who might be faster than he is, then he gets one of the other Bar X boys to take his stand in one of the alleys, ready to drop his opponent before he gets a chance to use his gun. I've seen it happen before – I know.'

Bob nodded his head slowly, musingly. So that was how it was done. Against men like Jeb and Joe, men who scarcely ever handled their guns, he would meet them face to face, knowing he could gun them down without any risk to himself. But if he was warned that he, Bob, was looking for him, he would do exactly as this old man said. He cursed himself inwardly for not having realized the danger before. Like the groom said, if he hadn't met up with him, he might

16

be dead before he got a chance at Duffield.

'All right, old-timer,' he said evenly. 'I take your point. Now will you tell me where Duffield is?'

'He's with the sheriff. He stopped off at Rowland's office on the way in. My guess is that Will is tellin' him not to make any trouble. That warnin' even though Rowland didn't know it now, could be the signin' of your death warrant.' He bent forward a little, obviously waiting for an answer.

'But I've been warned now.' He took back his pouch, pushed it into his pocket. 'I figure I may be able to lay a trap of my own.'

He heard the other's chuckle as he moved away, a faint sound in the darkness. It was followed by the scrape of a match as the oldster lit his cigarette. As he crossed swiftly to the other side of the street, he cast about him for the most likely place where a man might hide, waiting to cut down an unsuspecting man in the back, taking into account the direction from which Duffield would come from the sheriff's office. Almost at once, he spotted the dark mouth of the alley which ran back from the main street less than twenty yards away.

Pausing in the deep shadows of the boardwalk where the wooden overhang made it impossible for anyone watching to see him, he continued to keep an eye on the dark mouth of the alley. A minute passed, then another. There was still no movement in the blackness, nothing to indicate that a man might be standing there, well back from the road, ready to dry-gulch him the moment he moved out to challenge Duffield.

Could he have been mistaken? Maybe this was all guesswork on the part of that groom at the livery stable. Then he caught a sudden pale orange flare, just visible from where he stood. The hidden gunman had given himself away as he lit a cigarette, the flame reflected from the alley wall.

Moving quickly, now that he had the other's position, he

stepped aside from the doorway, his feet making no sound on the slatted wooden boards, made a wide circuit of the block, entering the alley from the rear. Now he could just make out the silent shape of the man, silhouetted against the brighter glow of the main street. He was lounging against the wall, perfectly relaxed, expecting no trouble, just waiting for the moment when he could shoot his victim in the back.

Cat-footing it along the alley, carefully working his way past piles of rubble, along the front of a shuttered feedstore, he came up behind the other before the gunhawk was aware of his presence. The man stiffened abruptly as the muzzle of the Colt was pushed hard into the small of his back.

'Just hold it right there,' he hissed softly. 'Make a move for your iron and I'll blow you apart.'

'What is this?' muttered the other hashly. 'A hold-up?'

'You know damned well it ain't.' Bob's laugh was harsh and brittle. 'Trouble is that your kind will never learn. You figure I don't know how it is that Charlie Duffield makes out against anyone who knows how to handle a gun. Have one of his pardners hide in an alley, ready to plug his opponent in the back.'

'You got this thing all wrong.' The other swallowed with a dry throat and made an attempt to bluster his way out of his present precarious position. This was clearly something which had never happened to him before and he did not quite know what to do about it. Without moving his thin lips, the other went on: 'Your name Bob Nevin?'

'That's right,' Bob said forcefully. 'The *hombre* who's been askin' around for Charlie Duffield. Reckon that's how you and Duffield got to hear of it and why he's decided to stake you out here to take care of me just in case I do look like beatin' him to the draw.'

'You've got this all wrong,' said the other. His voice rose

18

a little in pitch. Evidently he could already see himself being shot down by this man who stood behind him.

There was a sudden movement along the street. Bob jerked up his head, saw the man who came riding slowly along the middle of the wide street, knew instinctively that this was Charlie Duffield, the killer he had sworn to destroy. The man in front of him, evidently believing that this might be the last chance he would get to save himself, galvanized his body into action, tried to run forward out of the alley to yell a warning to the Bar X foreman. He had taken only one step when the butt of Nevin's Colt struck him a vicious blow behind the ear and he slumped sideways against the alley wall, crumpling slowly to the ground. There had been scarcely a sound and a swift glance showed Nevin that Duffield had heard nothing, suspected nothing as he came riding slowly forward, eyes flicking from one side of the street to the other. As he passed across a swathe of yellow light from one of the windows, Nevin saw the other stare straight at the alley where he stood, knew that the other was watching for a sign that his man was there, ready for trouble.

Nevin waited until the other had reined up his mount in front of the saloon and then stepped down, looping the reigns over the hitching rail. Then he stepped out of the shadows, his hands swinging loosely by his sides.

'Duffield!'

The other swung sharply, stared across at him and in the yellow light from the saloon, Bob was able to see the faint expression of surprise and fear that flashed across the foreman's thick features.

'Your dry-gulcher won't help you this time,' Nevin went on. 'He's lyin' back there in the alley, so it's just between you and me.'

'Your name Bob Nevin?'

'That's right. I've been lookin' for you in connection

with the killin' of Jeb Caldwell and Joe Fordham in twin Forks.'

'Way I hear it, it was a fair fight. Both of those *hombres* drew first on me.'

'Way I hear it, it was a mite different. Neither of those men were gunmen and they never had a chance against you.'

'Then I figure they shouldn't have called me out,' snarled the other. He kept his gaze fixed on Nevin, not once turning his head.

'You called them out,' Bob snapped. 'They had no other choice but to try to defend themselves.'

Duffield's eyes narrowed down as he swept the other intently. His face worked savagely as he stood close to the boardwalk and the thought of action was growing stronger in his gaze and the set of his mouth. 'So I killed 'em,' he said harshly. 'You callin' me out, Nevin?'

'That's right.' Bob nodded. 'Any time you care to make your play. This time though, you'll do it without the help of a man hidin' in the shadows.'

Duffield's tongue passed swiftly over his dry lips. Some of the boldness seemed to have gone from him as he stood there and his fingers, hovering near the butts of his guns, grew rigid and still.

'Well, what're you waitin' for? You suddenly gone yeller?' asked Bob tauntingly.

The other still hesitated. The truth of it was that he knew himself to be fast with a gun, but he had never stacked up against a man like this without having that extra help of a man stationed in one of the dark alleys. This man was no Jeb Caldwell or Joe Fordham. Bob began walking slowly towards the other, knowing that this, more than anything else, would prompt the other into action and force his hand.

Then, abruptly, without warning, a shot bucketed from

across the street, some twenty yards away. Bob caught the glare of orange light from the muzzle of the hidden gun, went down instinctively on his knees, drew and fired in a single motion, sending a bullet in the direction of the vivid stiletto of flame. He heard the slug smack against the wall of one of the buildings and then there was the unmistakable clatter of running feet, darting back along one of the alleys.

But Nevin scarcely noticed this. Whoever that hidden gunman had been, he had given Duffield the edge he needed to draw his own gun and start shooting. Bob swung swiftly, to cover the foreman, bringing up his gun, his finger tightening abruptly on the trigger, expecting to see the flash of gunfire from the other and feel the leaden impact of a slug burning its way into his body. But no bullet came.

Instead, he saw Duffield sliding to his feet, his Colt half drawn from its holster. He crumpled into a sitting position in the dust at the bottom of the steps leading up to the saloon, hung there as though reluctant to let go, then fell sideways on to his face as the doors of the saloon burst open and a crowd of men spilled out.

Beyond them, Bob saw the figure of Sheriff Rowland running along the sidestreet. His gun was out, the swathes of light from the windows on either side glinting off the metal as he ran. He came up to the inert figure of the Bar X foreman, bent and turned him over, then got to his feet and moved towards Bob Nevin.

There was a grim look on his face as he halted in front of the other, the gun in his hand covering Bob, the barrel not wavering by so much as an inch.

'I warned you about causin' trouble, Nevin,' he said tightly. 'Now drop that gun and shuck your gunbelt. I'm takin' you in for murder.'

For a long moment, Bob stared at him in surprise. Then he gasped out. 'Now see here, Sheriff. I didn't shoot Duffield. I'd called him out – sure, but before either of us drew, a shot came from the other side of the street.'

Rowland nodded slowly, disbelievingly, and there was a thin-lipped, sneering smile on his face. 'There are plenty of witnesses to the fact that you rode into town with the avowed intention of killin' Duffield. Looks to me like a clear-cut case. Only you shot him in the back without givin' him a chance to draw his gun. That ain't what I care to call a fair fight.' His thumb clicked back the hammer of his Colt. 'Now shuck that belt or I'll plug you here and now, without givin' you the benefit of any trial.'

Slowly, Bob unbuckled the gunbelt and let it drop into the dusty street. He was aware of the faces of the crowd watching him, of the looks on most of them. There were several of the Bar X crowd there, standing on the steps of the saloon and along the boardwalk and he heard the threatening mutter as they began to move forward.

'Why bother lockin' him up, Sheriff,' said one of them harshly. 'We know how to take care of killers like this *hombre*.'

For a moment Rowland hesitated, then he said evenly. 'I'm the law in Benson, Jorgens. I say that he's locked up until Judge Thorn gets here week after next. But I promise you that the trial will be short and swift. Then we'll string him up from the cottonwood yonder.'

'And if he ain't found guilty?' suggested another man. 'Reckon Old Man Sloan won't take kindly to havin' his foreman cut down in cold blood like this. He may decide to do somethin' about it himself.'

'Sloan ain't runnin' this town yet,' Rowland said thinly. 'Any of you boys want to start any trouble and you'll have me to deal with. Now get on with your drinkin' or ride on out of town.' There was a note of menace in his voice and Bob saw their glances fall away. Then most of them turned and went back into the saloon. Only three men moved off, cut their mounts from the rail, swung up into the saddle

22

and rode off into the darkness.

Rowland turned back to Bob. 'Now move on down the street to the jail, Nevin. Don't give me any trouble. I'm just waitin' to pull this trigger. If I did, it'd save me a heap of trouble.'

'Just a minute, Sheriff,' said Bob urgently. 'I want you to take a look in the mouth of that alley back yonder. Duffield had put one of his men there to shoot me in the back as soon as I called him. Seems that's the way he works when he knows he's up against somebody who can handle a gun. I knocked that dry-gulcher cold before steppin' out into the street.'

Rowland bit his lower lip, then called to one of the men standing on the boardwalk. 'Clem! Take a look in the alley yonder.'

The man moved off, came back a couple of minutes later. 'Ain't nobody there I can see, Sheriff,' he said evenly.

'Damn it all. I knocked him cold with my gunbutt. He's got to be there. He couldn't have come round so soon.'

'You callin' me a liar, mister?' snarled the other. He stepped forward, swung his clenched fist without warning. Taken by surprise, Bob had no chance to dodge the blow and reeled back as it struck him high on the side of the face, sending him staggering against one of the wooden uprights nearby. With an effort, he pulled himself upright, anger surging through him.

'All right, that's enough.' Rowland's gun covered him. 'Guess you'll say anythin' to get out of this.' Bending he picked up Bob's gun, opened it, sniffed at the barrel, then thrust it into his belt. 'One shot fired and recently,' he said, leaving Bob in no doubt as to the significance he put on that fact.

'Sure there is,' Bob said tensely. 'I told you that some-body shot from the other side of the street and I fired back.'

Sheriff Rowland said nothing more, but moved behind

him, prodded him in the back with his gun and thrust him forward. 'Get movin',' he said tightly. Over his shoulder, he called: 'Take Duffeld's body to the funeral home. If Herbie ain't up, knock him up from his bed.'

Nevin saw that it was useless for him to resist. Nobody in town would believe his story now. Whoever that killer had been, skulking there in the shadows, he would not come forward to save his life. Maybe if he had realized, in time, that the bullet had not been intended for him, but for Duffield, he might have stood a chance of being believed. But by loosing off that single shot, he had doomed himself.

Rowland prodded him with the gun all the way to the jail, forced him up the steps, through the outer office and along the narrow corridor that led to the cells at the rear.

'Inside,' said the other, unlocking one of the doors. Lowering his head a little, Nevin went in. Immediately, the door was slammed shut behind him and the heavy key turned in the lock. Rowland said tautly: 'If you want my advice, mister, better just stay here and don't try to give me any more trouble. Otherwise, I might just consider ridin' out of town and leavin' one of my deputies in charge. That crowd out there seemed to be in a pretty ugly mood tonight. They wouldn't think twice about busting you out of jail and puttin' a hempen rope around your neck and stretchin' it.'

Nevin said nothing, but went over to the low bunk and stretched himself out on it. The deep-seated weariness was back in his body now, suffused through every limb and he had a lot in his mind to think over. A few moments later, Rowland nodded to himself, went off along the passage. There was the hollow clang of the door at the far end closing.

CHAPTER TWO

TIME FOR GUNS

The sun was a burning disc in the cloudless heavens, not yet at its zenith but sending down a haze of heat that turned the small dust bowl into a cauldron, the rocks hot to the touch. Here, on the edge of the valley, there was no breeze and the still air blistered a man's face and seared all life from his lungs with every breath he managed to drag down into them. The fringe of dry grass and withered brush afforded little protection to the three men who lay inside the depression, their faces caked with the white dust, their lips cracked and dry, their eyes red-rimmed from the harsh, biting alkali which had worked its way between their lids.

High above them, invisible against the terrible glare of the sun, unless a man squinted his eyes, narrowing them down to mere slits, a small cloud of buzzards circled endless, like pieces of black cloth flapping against the mirror of the sky. They would occasionally descend, wheeling in slow, lazy arcs, and then rise again, not daring to come too close, knowing that the men below them were still alive, although it was doubtful if any of them would be by the time nightfall came and a cooler air swept over the valley.

The carcase of a dead steer lay on the side of the slope behind them, a few yards away and it was this which was attracting the circling buzzards. It had been shot less than two hours before. The three men, riding the boundary fence of the Circle Four ranch, had come on it shortly after it had been shot. More than fifty others, prime beef cattle, had been driven off, and they had spotted the dust cloud in the distance, heading out in the direction of the low hills that lay between the ranchland and the open desert.

The blizzard of lead which had come from the rocks on either side of them, had taken them completely by surprise, sent them diving for the only cover there was and less than fifteen seconds after they had scrambled down into the dust bowl, the shooting had spooked their horses, sent them racing into the desert.

Now they were pinned down here with the terrible heat increasing in intensity, slowly frying them, burning their necks and shoulders, drawing all of the moisture from their bodies, bringing with it the punishment of the damned. Their attackers were keeping out of sight among the tumbled boulders which overlooked the depression, knowing that they could afford to wait it out, that there was no need for them to take risks and expose themselves to any return fire. The blazing sun would do all that was necessary. Here, on the edge of the Badlands, with no water and the temperature going up every minute, five or six hours would be enough to send a man mad.

Bert Siegel rubbed the sweat from his eyes, brushed back the lank hair that fell over his forehead. He squinted up at the fiery sun, then squeezed his eyes tightly shut against the vicious glare.

'Why the hell don't they just rush us and have done with it?' he muttered through cracked lips. 'They must know they outnumber us by five to one. We don't stand a chance of gettin' away without horses.'.

'They don't want to lose any men if they can help it,' grunted Rod Evans. He knuckled the dust from his clear grey eyes. The shock of dark hair made him look younger than his twenty-nine years.

'What I don't figure, is why they hit us in the first place. This is Circle Four territory. And from what I saw, they don't look like ramrods from one of the other spreads.' Cal Fallon rolled over on to one elbow, sucking air into his lungs.

'They ain't.' Siegel spat dust from his mouth. He glanced down at the dried blood on his arm. 'I know that bunch. They're from the Mining Company. Vergil Clayton warned the cattlemen that if he caught any of their men on land he says belongs to the Corporation, he'd hang 'em from the nearest trees. Don't make no difference to him that this is legally Circle Four land. He reckons he's got the law backin' him and he aims to shoot down every man he finds on it.'

'Damn his soul to hell,' swore Fallon. He lifted his head cautiously, stared off into the rocks where the marksmen were hidden. 'You don't reckon he's there with 'em, do you?'

'So's you can get him in your sights?'

'You're damned right. I might figure it a worthwhile trade if I plugged him before they got me.'

Siegel rubbed the stubble on his face with the back of his hand, making a harsh, scraping sound that rasped in the clinging stillness. 'I wonder where they have their horses stashed?'

'Not a chance,' said Evans. 'They're too far away for us to reach 'em, even if they haven't got a guard on 'em, which they have.'

Siegel nodded, recognising the truth in the other's words. He lowered his head until it touched his outstretched arm, closing his eyes. There was no feeling left in his mind now which was curious, as he had felt an almost insane anger against these killers when they had first driven

27

them into the dubious shelter of these rocks. But over the long, heat-stretched minutes the feeling had faded until it had all been burned out of him by the sunglare. He knew that in the next hour or so, if they stayed alive that long, they would find a bullet infinitely preferable to the heat. He wondered if it had occured to the other two that this was the last day of their lives, that death would find them before sundown.

It all seemed so very unfair that fate should have chosen this death for them, for none of them had done anything to deserve it. They had broken no law except for that which Clayton claimed for himself. They had merely been minding their own business out here on the edge of the Circle Four spread. Edging forward a little, he parted the tufts of dry grass and squinted through. The nearest stretch of cover lay more than a hundred yards from the circular depression and every inch of the open ground was covered by the gunmen. It would be sheer suicide to try to cross it. The thought was a bitter thing to accept.

As the minutes dragged by and the sun climbed to its zenith, the burning pressure became a roasting hell that ate at their flesh, brought the sweat streaming into their eyes, eyes which burned and itched intolerably from the vicious glare and the irritating grains of dust and sand which had worked their way under the lids.

'I'm goin' to try for those rocks yonder,' Evans croaked finally. His face was flushed, his eyes brighter than normal.

Realizing that the other was out of his mind, Siegel lunged to one side, caught at the other's arm as he struggled forward. 'Don't be a goddamned fool, Rod. You'll never make it. They're just lyin' in wait out there, hopin' that you'll do somethin' like that so they can pick you off like a sittin' duck.'

'What else is there to do? Stay here and roast to death?' Wriggling forward on his stomach, the other reached the lip of the depression, paused for a moment and then slithered over it, dropping down to the other side, head and shoulders low, the rest of his body pressed tightly into the dusty earth.

'Goddamn,' muttered Fallon. He jerked up his Colt, ready to give covering fire as Evans snaked forward through the clumps of dry, brown grass. From behind one of the boulders, Siegel peered into the sunhaze, winced as rifles cracked from the bushes a hundred yards away. Through slitted eyes he saw Evans jerk, open his mouth to yell, then get crazily to his feet, swaying slightly. There was blood on the front of his shirt and his eyes were wide open, staring directly at the men who had shot him, although it was doubtful if he saw any of them. With a tremendous effort of will and strength, he lifted his right hand, the sweat standing out on his face, lips twisted in agony, the veins on his neck showing under the tanned skin. He tottered forward for a couple of paces, then his finger jerked on the trigger and he loosed off one shot, the sound bucketing through the ensuing stillness. From somewhere in the distance a man gave up a hoarse, loud cry as the bullet found its mark. Then Evans dropped forward on to his face, arms outflung, the gun slipping from his nerveless fingers, half-burying itself in the sand.

Within seconds of him going down, six men rose up from the brush and began their run towards the depression. Propping himself on one elbow, Siegel began firing wildly. The blurred shapes of the men danced and swayed in front of his vision and it was almost impossible to take a proper aim. The burning heat of the sun had already taken its toll of his strength and sight.

Beside him, cursing wildly, Fallon emptied his gun at the attackers, bent his head as he pulled cartridges from his belt and thumbed them into the empty chambers. Siegel kept up a steady fire, saw one of the men go down on one knee, clutching at a torn shoulder. Another threw up his arms with a great cry and fell backwards as the heavy slug took him high in the chest. Blood welled from his mouth as he dropped, stretching out his legs convulsively before lying still.

More rifles cracked from the bushes behind him. Then something scorched along the side of his skull and he fell forward into darkness.

Rock Hempel strode slowly to the edge of the hollow, stood on the crumbling earth and stared down at the two men lying in the sand. 'Both of these men are from the Circle Four,' he said sharply. 'Better check that other *hombre* out there.' He jerked a thumb towards Evans, lying face down in the scorched earth.

One of the men went back, turned the dead Circle Four rider over, let his arm drop. 'He's dead,' he said quietly.

'But these two are still alive,' muttered another man, bending over Siegel and Fallon. 'One's got a crease along his skull and the other has a hole in his shoulder.'

Hempel nodded. He was a tall, squat man, with sharp, black eyes and a body which looked as though it had been hewn out of granite. 'We'll hang 'em both, like Clayton said.' he grunted. 'That should be sufficient warnin' to Nevin that we mean business. Maybe the next time he's told to get off the range, he'll do it.'

The other laughed harshly, took his canteen from his belt and poured a little of the water over Siegel's face. Coughing and spluttering, Siegel came round, water plastering his hair close to his scalp. The water washed away most of the blood, leaving the wound raw and angry-looking. He opened his eyes, blinked several times against the harsh glare, then found himself looking into the pitiless eyes of the men who stood in a circle around him, knew he could expect no mercy from any of them.

'On your feet,' snapped Hempel. He lowered the barrel

of his Colt until it was lined up on the other's chest, his thumb clicking back the hammer.

Slowly, his head swimming, Siegel staggered upright. The rocky depression seemed to swing and sway about him and a wave of nausea surged up into his stomach. Out of the corner of his blurred vision, he saw that Cal Fallon had been hauled to his feet, that he was now hanging limply between two of the men.

'What do you figure on doin' with us now?' Siegel asked through dry, slack lips.

Hempel grinned viciously. 'We're goin' to make certain that there ain't any more trouble from the Circle Four riders,' he said harshly. Turning his head, he nodded towards the solitary cottonwood that grew out of the arid soil a couple of hundred yards away. 'Take 'em over there and string 'em up. Reckon that ought to be fair enough warnin' to anybody who wants to tangle with the Company.'

'You got any complaint against Nevin, why don't you take it up with him,' Siegel mumbled. 'No call for you to drygulch us. We just work for him. He gives the orders.'

'Trouble is, he don't take kindly to any other warnings we give. Seems we got to do somethin' more to make him realize that we really mean business.' The other stepped forward and ground the muzzle of his gun into Siegel's ribs. 'Just unfortunate that you three happened along when you did. Fate sure played a rotten deal on you.'

Siegel was caught and he knew there was now no way of winning free of this deal. Grabbing his arms he was dragged over the rough ground to the cottonwood, and stood under it while one of the men went for a couple of horses. Unable to struggle, he was hoisted on to the back of one of them and his hands were tied tightly behind him, the thongs biting deeply and painfully into his wrists. Hempel had taken his lariat from his saddlehorn and tossed it expertly over one projecting limb of the tree, settling the noose around Siegel's neck. Fallon was set on the other horse, two men holding him there, his head slumping forward on to his chest. He was barely conscious, his eyes lidding and closing. Not until the noose was placed around his neck did he seem to realize the full deadliness of his position. Then he jerked himself upright in the saddle, turning his head from right to left, eyes wide, staring at the men standing around him before throwing his head back a little as far as the tension on the rope would allow him, peering up at the branch over his head, the riata slung over it.

'Just so long as you know what's happenin' to you,' rasped Hempel. He took a couple of steps back, nodded to the men hanging on to the ropes. Siegel felt the noose tighten around his neck, cutting off his air. Lights began to flash brilliantly in front of his eyes and there was a thudding roar in his ears which threatened to drown out everything else. Involuntarily, his legs began to twitch and kick. Then, at a sudden shout from Hempel, two men slashed at the horses' rumps. Snorting, they bounded forward. . . .

It was almost dusk when Ben Nevin and five of his men reached the spot where Seigel and the others had been shot down. When the three riders had failed to return that afternoon, Nevin had decided to go look for them, knowing that with the trouble brewing over the Mining Company's claims to his land, anything might have happened to them.

They found Evan's body first, lying sprawled in the sand close to the spot where the ground dipped abruptly into the dust bowl. Dismounting, Nevin walked over to the dead man, turned him over and stared down into the still face and the open, sightless eyes. His lips were drawn together into a tight, grim line as he straightened and looked up at the mounted men.

'He's been dead for some hours,' he said dully. 'Get him up on one of the horses and we'll take him back with us.'

'Where are Siegel and Fallon?' asked one of the other men.

'They'll be around here someplace. Spread out and search for them.' Nevin climbed into the saddle as the men spread out and began their search. They moved warily now, knowing that something had happened to these men which could also strike at them if they were not sufficiently cautious. All three men knew how to handle their guns, yet they had been cut down in this god-forsaken spot, and were all dead, unless the two of them had been taken prisoner.

Five minutes later, the slowly-swinging bodies of the two men, suspended from the cottonwood, were discovered. Seated in the saddle, Nevin watched silently with bleak eyes as Siegel and Fallon were cut down. He said tightly after a pause: 'Clayton did this. He swore he'd kill any men he found if I didn't give in to him.'

'You goin' to let him get away with it? If you don't stop him now, he'll just go on until we're all killed.'

Nevin lifted his head and met the other's head-on stare. He could guess at the thoughts in the other's mind which had prompted that question. 'Three of our men killed, shot down from ambush and then two of them hanged. I don't have the men to fight Clayton and he knows it.'

'What about the other ranchers who're threatened? Won't they side with you if you make 'em see that divided they don't have a chance?'

Nevin shook his head wearily. He watched as the two men were cut down and draped over the backs of a couple of horses. 'Maybe if Bob was here he might know how to fight Clayton.'

'I wonder.' The man's eyes held a curious, far-away look. 'One man won't make all that much difference, whether or not he's fast with a gun. But I reckon you'll have to do some-thin'. The boys will run if you don't.'

'They'll run out of weakness. Let 'em run. I don't want men like that.'

The man shook his head emphatically. 'Better think this thing out straight, Mister Nevin. I like workin' for you. You give us good pay, good food and the work is good. But that counts for nothin' if you have a man like Clayton, sendin' out his gunhands to shoot us down without warnin' like he did Siegel and the others. If the men start runnin' it'll leave you stripped.'

'We have friends. The law is on our side. This is my land and I aim to keep it, Clayton or not.'

'But without men and guns you don't stand a chance. This was meant as the first warnin'. My guess is that Clayton will be ridin' in to have a word with you pretty soon. He'll make you an offer and if you don't take it, then the next time it'll be the ranch he'll fire and he'll destroy everybody in it. Bob's too far away for him to help.'

Nevin rubbed the back of his hand across his face. In spite of the coolness of the night air, there was sweat on his forehend, trickling down his grizzled cheeks and blending with the alkali dust to form itching channels on his face. For the present, all of the vitality seemed to have gone from him and he had nothing particular on his face, no emotion, no anger even. It was blank, as if his mind was a thousand miles away, as though he had just wakened from a deep, hard sleep and not yet succeeded in dragging his mind back to reality.

Inwardly, he still had his deep-seated anger; and he wanted to use it. But commonsense told him that it would be impossible to fight Clayton at the moment with the few men he had.

'Let's get back to the ranch,' he said shortly. 'It's gettin' late and we'll have to bury the boys.'

'You goin' to send for Bob then?' There was something more than just a question in the other's tone. He looked at

Nevin with a bright-sharp glance.

'I'll think about it. Last I heard of him he was in Twin Forks lookin' up a couple of friends of his. Could be if he knew the trouble we was in, he'd come ridin' fast enough.'

'We sure need somebody around here like Bob,' nodded the other. 'Though I'm still doubtful if he can help us now. Clayton has been building up his force of rannies for too long, keeping it a secret from most of the folk in the valley. When he first came, nobody figured that he'd be able to turn the law to his own ends like this, but I reckon with the circuit judge in his pocket, he can do anythin'.'

Ben Nevin showed him his thin, wintery smile, then pulled hard on the reins, turning his horse's head, kicking in with the rowels of his spurs, urging the animal forward. The man seated quietly in the saddle behind him, stared after him for a long moment, then shrugged, gave the necessary orders to the rest of the men.

It was dark when the crew rode in with the three dead men, whirling into the courtyard and stirring the grey dust which lay on the hard, sun-baked ground. Lighting down, they peeled their gear from their mounts, turned the horses loose into the corral and then dispersed to the bunkhouse. Ben Nevin walked into the house, feeling weary in both body and spirit. The day's latest development had only served to show him how weak he really was. Clayton was going to call the tune here in the valley and as far as Nevin could see, there was no man strong enough to stop him. He had laid his plans well, paying good money to bring in the deadliest gunslingers in the entire territory. These were all men who lived outside of the law, who cared nothing for human life and were ready to kill so long as they received their due payment. His own men could not possibly stand up to gunslingers such as these, hard cases whose only law was the gun. He had hired his men to herd cattle, mend fences and ride the perimeter watching for strays, men who could handle a branding iron, turn their hands to any odd chore about the place. When he had taken them on, there had been no sign of trouble in the valley. Not until the mining company had moved in, backed by claims which they stated were lawful, giving them control of the land for their development. Ben did not doubt that these claims were illegal, that if they were taken in front of one of the law courts back east, they would be repudiated at once and the mining company ordered to cease operations forthwith. But Clayton had been hired by the company to see to it that nobody got the chance to bring the claim to court. He had got hold of a crooked judge and that had been enough. Any attempt to obtain justice in the court held in Aracoa, the nearest town, had resulted in defeat.

The confines of the house oppressed him and he went out on to the porch, stared out at the dark wave of the trees that hung poised over the tops of the hills around the edges of the valley. He had his eyes wide open and starlight danced in them. The moon had just lifted, round and huge and yellow above the highest peaks, although the valley itself was still dark, with only the first flush of moonlight on the higher reaches of the hills. This was the place he had known for more years than he could remember. He had brought Susan here more than twenty years before. The first cabin had been a makeshift erection of logs hewn from the tall cedars and pines that crowded the hills. Then he had started his herd, watched it build up and grow with his dreams. Bob had been born in the ranch-house on a sun-blistering night with the crickets buzz-sawing out in the tall grass and the horses moving restlessly in the confines of the corral. Now Bob was out there somewhere and he had not seen him for almost four years. As for Susan, he had buried her on the low knoll overlooking the ranch where the warm sunlight and the wind might be her companions in her eternal rest. Almost unconsciously, his glance drifted in that direction. Then he stiffened abruptly. He saw the dust kicked up by the approaching riders before the sound reached him, drifting down on the night breeze.

It was part of Vergil Clayton's bunch, he guessed. He had expected the other to wait until the next day before riding in to try to talk him into selling the spread. Now it seemed that Clayton was a man who wanted to hustle things along, to strike while the iron was hot.

Miles Thornton came out of the bunkhouse across the courtyard, glanced up as he caught the oncoming echoes of the riders, then walked quickly over to the house.

'Party ridin' in, boss.' he said softly. 'Reckon it could be Clayton?'

'I'm sure it is.' There was a growing hardness in Nevin's tone. 'And I can figure why he's here. He doesn't mean to give me a chance to forget what happened to Siegel and the others. He wants to force me into sellin' the spread.' He thinned his lips into a grim smile. 'Well he's goin' to find that this is only goin' to make me more determined to stay here. All I've got is in the ranch and I don't intend that a low-down snake like Clayton is goin' to get it, or the mining company he works for.'

'Want me to get the rest of the boys? Reckon we could hold 'em off for a while if we barricaded ourselves in the house.'

'No.' Ben's tone was sharp. 'He won't want to make trouble tonight. I'll just get an ultimatum. I know Clayton and how he thinks. But I want you to do somethin' for me, Miles.'

'Sure.' The other eyed him quizzically.

'Get your bronc out of the corral and ride for Twin Forks. Try to find Bob and tell him what's happenin' here. We may be able to hold Clayton off for a few more days, maybe even a couple of weeks or so. But after that, I'm not so sure.'

'It's more'n a two-day ride out to Twin Forks. Maybe he ain't there any longer and—'

'Then start askin' around for him. Get in touch with Jeb Caldwell or Joe Fordham. They may know where he's headed.'

Miles nodded quickly, made his way over to the corral, spurs dragging in the dust. Less than five minutes later, he rode out of the courtyard, heading in the opposite direction to the oncoming men. Clayton may smell the other's dust when he arrived, Nevin thought, but he would not be suspicious. His glance swept the yard as he stood there on the porch, saw the shadows of the men in the doorway of the bunkhouse. Evidently they guessed that there might be a show-down here and were wondering who would come out of it the best. The sound of the advancing party was loud now and a moment later, they broke timber and came riding along the wider stretch of trail towards the courtyard. Nevin noticed the buckboard in the lead, with two men flanking it a little way behind, and beyond them perhaps fifteen mounted men who swung about and remained in the saddle as Vergil Clayton brought the buckboard to a halt in front of the ranch and stepped down.

CHAPTER THREE

CLASH BY NIGHT

Standing in the dust just below the porch, Clayton brought his gaze to a full-centred aim at Nevin. There was a faintly cynical smile on his face as he said: 'Mind if I have a talk, Nevin. I figure we've got some important business to discuss.'

Nevin raised his brows a little, lit the cigarette he had built and blew smoke out into the still air. He tried to frame something in his mind that would make it clear to the other he knew who had been responsible for the killing of his men that day, but could think of nothing sufficiently scathing and merely answered: 'I don't figure we've got anythin' to talk about, Clayton. But if you want to say some-thin', step inside.'

The other paused, swept his gaze around the silent court-yard, at the corral and then in the direction of the bunkhouse. Finally, when he was satisfied that his men vould be able to take care of any trouble that might begin, he nodded, stepped up on to the porch and followed Ben inside.

In the front room, he faced the other across the table, said in his calm, self-certain way: 'Don't you know when you're beat yet? I've made you a perfectly good offer for this land. So far, you've refused even to discuss it. But after what happened today, you can't afford not to talk it over.'

'What is supposed to have happened today?' Nevin enquired. He laid his level gaze on the other, his mouth tight.

'You know damned well what I'm talkin' about. Three of your men were shot by outlaws on the edge of the valley.'

'How do you know that?'

'There's plenty of talk,' replied the other softly. He did not betray anything on his face as he took out a cheroot, lit it and let the smoke trickle in twin streams through his nostrils.

'There's more than talk,' Nevin said tightly. He felt the anger growing in him, but forced it down under control, exercising his iron will not to show the other that he was edgy. 'I happen to know that it was a bunch of your hired killers who did it.'

Just for a second, the mask of indifference on the other's face slipped, then it was back again and he said softly: 'You won't find it easy to prove that. Now don't you see sense? Soon I'll stop talkin' and start tellin' you. A few more encounters and you'll find that those men you have left will just take the trail over the hill and keep on ridin'. No man likes to work for a spread where he don't get any protection.'

'That a threat, Clayton?' asked Nevin, an angry glitter in his eyes.

'Let's say that it's just a friendly warnin' at the moment.' The other grinned viciously. 'You saw the men who rode with me tonight. I could get three times that number in a week or so and then you'd have no chance at all against me. We don't want any unpleasantness in the valley, but the Company is determined to enforce the law here, and the law says that the valley belongs to us. You took it over some years ago, but you laid no formal claim to it and it belongs to the first person to sign a claim on it.'

'You know damned well that this claim of yours isn't worth the paper that it's written on,' said Nevin harshly. 'Once we take it to the court in Dallas, it'll be tossed out and you'll soon find that this land belongs to those who settled it after the war.'

'I doubt it,' answered Clayton. 'Your kind is always full of bluster, but when it comes to a showdown you'll do nothin'. It's just a way you try to cover your weakness.'

Nevin's expression again grew solid and resisting. He put his glance on the other, waited for a moment, then said: 'You're wastin' your time tryin' to scare me, Clayton. If you try to fight me, you may win in the end, but you'll lose more of your men than you can afford.'

Clayton smiled a thin, wintery smile. 'My outfit is waitin' outside. How far do you think you could fight them if I gave the order to attack?'

'You talk too much,' Nevin said thinly. 'Step back and draw now if you care to risk your luck.'

The other shook his head. 'I've warned you before, Nevin. I pick my fights when and where I please.'

Nevin felt the anger burn through him. 'Then you'd better pick this one now,' he muttered, his right hand hovering close to the butt of the gun in his belt.

'I'm not goin' to repeat myself, Nevin. You've got a couple of weeks in which to make up your mind. Either you sell and move out peaceful, or we have to get tough and if that happens, you're finished.' Clayton's cheek muscles were bunched under the skin and there was a tightness around his eyes. Nevin was well aware of the emotions that were running deep in the man, matching his own; and also that the scene could end there and then if Clayton had as much brutality in him as he tried to make others believe. All he had to do was lift his voice and bring the rest of his crew in there – and the whole thing would be over. For a moment, Nevin thought that this was what might indeed happen. But the other dallied with his thoughts, made up his mind, and said sharply: 'Two weeks, Nevin. Then I come ridin'.'

He backed to the door, keeping his glance on Nevin, not trusting him. He went down the steps into the courtyard, called to his men, mounted on to the buckboard and sent the whip slashing over the backs of the horses in the traces. Nevin walked over to the door, stood watching the bunch ride out.

Hank, the cook, came over, stood quiet. At last he said: 'He try to freeze you out, boss?'

With an effort, Nevin pulled his thoughts back. 'He tried,' he said tautly. 'But we'll see. We'll see.'

Hank stood there for several moments, then finally drifted back to the bunkhouse. Nevin did not go back into the house at once, but remained on the porch, watching the moonlight flood slowly down into the valley, chasing the shadows. It was a cold, yellow light, matching the chill in his own mind. Would Miles find Bob in time? he wondered. It was so long since, he and his son had met, that he wasn't sure if he would know the boy if he met him face to face. What changes would these intervening years have wrought in Bob? Quite suddenly, he realized that there were a great many things he did not know about his own son.

Not more than fifteen minutes after he had ridden out of the Circle Four ranch, Vergil Clayton hauled hard on the reins, bringing the buckboard to a halt. From this point, he knew they were out of sight of anyone down on the ranch.

'Eaton and Cody.' He waited impatiently while the two riders broke out of the group and walked their mounts forward.

'Yes, boss.'

42

'When we were ridin' down to the ranch, I spotted a rider high-tailin' it out. He kicked up plenty of dust, so my guess is that Nevin has sent one of his men for help.'

'Ain't anybody who can help him,' said Elton harshly. 'Those other ranchers are too goddamned busy tryin' to look after themselves to worry about Nevin.'

'Maybe. But in my position you don't take chances. I want you two to ride after that *hombre* and see that he doesn't get to wherever it is he's headed.'

'You want him back dead or alive?' queried Cody. He fingered his gunbutt meaningly.

'Means little to me which way you do it.'

'Could be that he'll backtrack once he hits the top of the hill yonder,' said Elton musingly.

'Then it's up to you to find out,' snapped Clayton. 'Don't waste time sittin' here talkin'. Ride out now.'

Elton nodded, wheeled his mount. Cody cut after him, swinging up off the main trail until they were lost to view of the rest of the men.

Half an hour later, they were cutting up through a tangled area of coarse brush and thorn, with clumps of Spanish sword making the going slow and difficult for the horses. They had spotted the faint trail that led up through the tall hills and on two occasions, Elton had dismounted, lit a match and bent low to examine the trail, picking out the faint hoofprints of a man riding fast. By midnight, they were following a trail that wound and twisted endlessly through towering thickets which barred their way at every turn.

Grumbling, Cody said: 'Why don't we make camp here and follow this *hombre* in the daylight? It's too damned easy to miss the trail in this moonlight.'

'Unless we keep close on his heels, we may loose him,' muttered Elton. He knuckled the dust from his eyes. 'You heard what Clayton said.'

43

'Sure, and by now he'll be lyin' in his bed while we have to spend most of the night trackin' through this territory.'

'We keep ridin',' said the other harshly. 'If he makes camp, so much the better for us. We'll just take him and then head back.'

Cody muttered under his breath, but said nothing more. They rode through a maze of rocky gulches where the flooding moonlight threw long shadows over the uneven ground, slashing it in a glare of black and white. Coming out of a shallow ravine, they found that the ground opened out and they rode as hard as they dared, watchful for gopher holes which could snap a horse's leg like a matchstick if they went down into one on the run. The punishing pace was hard on their mounts, but they had withstood worse deprivations.

Around a humped bend, a small creek came into view, the rippling surface of the swift-running water glistening in the moonlight. The horses, their ears eagerly forward, cut straight across the grey-brown earth towards the water. Elton lifted his weary body from the saddle, dropped to the bank of the creek and let his mount drink while he built himself a smoke. Cody stretched himself like a cat, then knelt, cupped his hands and began to drink, rubbing the water over his dusty face, feeling the mask crack as the water soaked into it, burning his scorched flesh underneath.

Flicking the water from his hands, he straightened up. Glancing at the other he said: 'Who do you reckon this *hombre* is we're trailin'?'

Elton shrugged. 'Could be any of Nevin's hands. Reckon we won't know for sure until we catch up with him.'

'Sure, but why is he headed this way? Ain't no ranches in this direction. It just runs out over the desert, clear to the north for fifty miles or more.'

Elton gave a quick nod. The thought had occurred to him earlier. He had been expecting their quarry to turn off, make a wide detour perhaps, before heading back in the direction of the ranches which bordered on the Circle Four. But they had been trailing him now for close on three hours and he was still apparently headed north, out into the stretching desert which ran on for close on fifty miles. Another thought struck him at that moment. He said thinly: 'If he is headed that way, this is the last water on the way. Reckon we'd better fill up the canteens. It's a long way across the Badlands.'

Squatting on his heels, Elton let his gaze move over the small clearing on the edge of the stream. Some distance away, perhaps thirty yards, he noticed where the grass had been trampled down and guessed that their man had forded the creek at that point, riding up into the rugged boulders which lay beyond. In the moonlight, the rocks shone with a faint, eerie light, standing out clearly against the darker night sky beyond. He watched Cody move back to the stream, dip his bandanna into the water and wring it out before placing it on the back of his neck. 'We're close,' said Cody, glancing at the grass. 'He can't be more'n a couple of miles in front. I figure he ain't hurryin' none. Maybe reckons that he got clear away without bein' spotted.'

'That suggests he's got a long distance to cover,' mused Elton. He drew the smoke from the cigarette down into his lungs, let it go in short puffs through his lips.

'You figure he might turn and fight when we catch up with him?' For a moment there was something unholy in the other's voice, a sadistic note that did not pass unnoticed by Elton. He tightened his lips a little. He had been warned about this man, about his past record. They said that he had spent some years with the Apache Indians, that he knew many of their ways.

'If he does, we know what to do.' He drew slowly on his cigarette, watched the glowing tip for a moment. Then he flicked it away, pulled the long-barrelled Colt from its holster and spun it for a moment by the trigger guard before thrusting it back into leather again. 'Let's move out.'

They splashed over the shallow stream, followed the tracks on the other side where they showed up clearly in the soft, moist earth. Elton pointed down to them, saw Cody nod his head in understanding. From the top of the low rise, their quarry had slanted downward again, cutting through a wide belt of timber, keeping close to the stream as it wound through the trees. Under the canopy of leaves and branches that were closely intertwined over their heads, they were forced to ride slowly. Little moonlight succeeded in penetrating the thick overhead canopy and there were twisting creepers which could throw a horse easily at every step.

They made sharp switchbacks as the trail wound in and out of the timber, still climbing, but as they neared the top of the rise, the trees grew less dense and eventually, they came out into the open and were able to look back and see the stream down below them, gleaming faintly where the moonlight caught it. Beyond it, the huge twisted rock formations through which they had ridden earlier tumbled down against the stream, full of moonlight and shadow. There was no movement there as far as they could see and in the other direction, out to where the flatness of the Badlands stretched to a featureless horizon, glowing faintly in the cold moonlight, there was nothing to be seen that gave them any indication of the presence of the man they were hunting.

Out there in the treacherous alkali a man would have to ride slowly, Elton reflected. It was also possible that the other would make camp there, where he could keep a watch on the trail for some distance. He had half expected to find that the other had made camp beside the stream for that would be the last water he would see before he got to the other side of the desert. If the other had any sense and knew this country, he would have made early camp, rested his mount, so that he could make the journey over the Badlands in a single trip. Doing it any other way could easily lead to disaster.

They moved their horses down the slope which began to narrow into a natural funnel channelling them out into the desert. Out in the Badlands, the chill wind, which had not affected them among the protection of the trees, cut through their clothing, freezing the blood in their veins. The desert was a place of extremes. Burning with a blistering, fiery heat during the day and chilled by the icy wind at night.

Daylight was beginning to show in the east while they were still making their way through the alkali. Both of their mounts were beginning to feel the strain of the night's journey now. The caustic dust worked its way into their feet, irritating and laming. In spite of this, they forced the animals on at a swift gallop.

The tall rocks which jutted out from the far edge of the valley were clean and white in the early morning sunlight, but the desert that lay beyond them was still in deep shadow, almost the whole of the way across. Seated with his back against one of the boulders, Miles Thornton looked at the stretching black shadow beneath him and thought: Whoever they are, they will have to come this way and they'll be rushing this thing, hoping to take me by surprise.

He had spotted the cloud of dust in the distance less than half an hour before, knew what it betokened. Something had happened to make Clayton suspicious and he had sent some of his men after him.

Nursing his Winchester, he peered through the narrow groove in the rocks in front of him, watching for the first sign of the oncoming men. Around him, he could feel the dampness of the rocks and the early morning stillness lay over everything. Not a single sound broke the silence and he could feel the growing tightness in himself and just telling himself to sit back and relax was not enough. If there was quite a bunch of men trailing him, then his chances of getting out of here alive were short. Maybe it would have been best to force his mount on despite the lameness caused by the alkali. But he knew that now it was much too late. He could not hope to stay ahead of these men for more than an hour with his horse in its present condition. He would have been forced to stop and fight sometime; and this was probably the best defensive position he would ever find along this trail. At least, he ought to have the advantages of surprise, for none of these men would expect him to stay and fight.

Narrowing his eyes, he peered into the dimness, suddenly picked out the shapes of the two riders moving towards him. They were still a quarter of a mile off, but even at that distance, he thought he recognized them as two of Clayton's men. So he had not been mistaken after all. His fingers tightened around the stock of the Winchester and he placed the barrel carefully in the 'V' of the rocks, sighting along it, drawing a bead on the leading man's chest. He remained in that position for several minutes, lowering the sights slowly as the men came closer. They were, he saw, going to enter the narrow cut less than a hundred yards from his vantage point. From that distance, it would be virtually impossible for him to miss.

Cody and Elton, he thought grimly to himself now that he was just able to make out their faces clearly. Two of Clayton's hired killers. Maybe two of the men who had been in that party which had bushwhacked Siegel and the boys, shooting them down without warning. He felt the slow burn of anger inside him. Why not just pull the trigger now and be done with it? he thought savagely. It would be no worse a chance than that which they had given those other Circle Four riders, innocent men going about their lawful business.

But there was something in him which would not allow him to shoot down a man in cold blood, even a killer such as the man whose body was now squarely in his sights. His forefinger was light against the tightness of the trigger as he steeled himself to wait for a few more seconds. The men came forward slowly now, obviously wary, their heads turning as they flicked their gaze from side to side, alert for possible danger.

The two men were almost level with him now, would come no nearer. Sharply, he called out: 'Throw up your hands and hold it right there! Both of you!'

Reaction was immediate. Even as the echoes of his words were still bouncing back from the towering rock formations on either side of the trail, the two men hauled back on the reins, their mounts rearing sharply. Instinctively, he squeezed the trigger, saw the leading man fall drunkenly from the saddle, twisting a little as he went down. The second man, swinging his leg from the stirrup, holding himself close to his horse's body like an Indian brave, urged his mount along the trail, turning it into the rocks some seventy yards away.

Switching targets, Thornton sent two shots after him, saw the horse stumble as one of the slugs hit it, but it did not go down, miraculously maintaining its balance before it vanished into the rocks. The first man had hit the ground hard, as his mount had bolted, wounded, but not killed. Before Thornton could get off another shot at him, he had rolled out of sight into the cover of the boulders nearby.

Hell, how could he possibly have missed at that distance? he thought savagely. If only he had fired without giving fair warning, one of those men would have been dead by now, possibly the other. As it was, they were still dangerous, crouched down in the rocks, able to fire at him from two directions. Now the advantage lay with them. He studied the terrain in front of him thoughtfully. He was, if anything, slightly higher than either of the two men and beyond their positions, thick pines ran into the open ground off the trail. For the second time, Thornton was forced to settle down to wait, but this time, he knew the full fear of the deadliness of his position. The men he now faced were seasoned, hardened killers. They knew the tricks of their profession. He felt the first twinge of doubt in his mind as the silence grew long and there was no movement from the other edge of the trail.

Acting on impulse, he aimed quickly at the spot where the uninjured man had gone to cover, clinging to his mount. That would have been Cody, was the thought that went through his mind, the man who had lived, so they said, among the Apache for some years. He loosed off a couple of shots, spacing them one either side of the spot where he guessed the other ought to be.

Now wait for it, he thought tightly. If he's going to make a move, he'll make it now. A Springfield opened up on his right where the wounded man was hidden. The bullets ricochetted off the rocks a few feet away, causing him to flinch momentarily, but not to take his gaze off the spot where Cody was lying in wait. He guessed that Elton had opened up to give his partner the chance to move into a better position.

A second later, Cody made his move, darting with his head well down from one of the rocks high up the slope, higher than Thornton had been expecting. The other must have worked his way up the slope without being seen. For a moment, Thornton felt a wave of panic race through him as he sought desperately to bring the Winchester to bear on the running, leaping figure. He fired one shot, saw the puff of powdered stone where the slug hit, then fired again.

Cody went down, sprawling his full length on a rough slide of loose earth. His forward momentum carried him out of sight behind a huge boulder and it was impossible to say whether he had been hit or whether he had deliberately dived those last few yards in anticipation of the second slug he knew to be on its way.

All of this went through Thornton's mind as he pushed himself forward against the hard rock and wiped the trickle of sweat from his forehead with the back of his sleeve. He concluded: Whatever happens, I know where he is now and I've got to keep him pinned down there. He won't be able to make it back up that slope, it's too goddamned steep and rough for him to make it before I get a bead on him.

A swift glance to his left, down the slope and then he was moving behind the cover of the rocks. Raising his head slowly, he glanced down at Cody's hiding place from a different angle but could still see no sign of the gunman. Had the other somehow managed to slip away without being seen? Or had that last shot killed him? It was just possible that he was lying dead behind the boulders, but at that moment, Thornton was not a man to take unnecessary chances. Risking a shot from Elton's position, he ran for the rocks on the edge of the trail, paused crouching down for a moment, then got his legs braced beneath him, laid down his Winchester on the ground and pulled the Colt from its holster. The rifle was of little use for in-fighting such as he intended now. Another second and then he hurled himself forward, over the open stretch of the trail, towards the rocks on the far side. A single shot rang out from the gully where Elton was lying. The slug kicked up a spurt of dust a few inches behind Thornton's feet. Another whined over his head and ricochetted off the crest of a rock as he veered to his right, hit the ground hard and went down. Pressing himself close to the dirt, he exhaled slowly. His heart was thudding madly against his ribs, the blood pounding in his temples. Now they both ought to know where he was. Inching his way forward, he crawled along a sharply-angled gully, reached the top of the fold in the ground, lifted his head an inch at a time and peered cautiously around him in the pale dawn light. He heard the ominous click of a rifle bolt behind drawn back, levering the bullet into the breech, swung his head quickly in the direction of the sound. He would have to go a little more around, he reflected, before he was able to catch sight of Cody. Remembering the gunman's reputation, he hesitated for a moment. If his earlier shot had not hit him, the other could be playing possum, waiting for him to show himself, ready to put a bullet through his head the minute he crawled into view.

Lying on his stomach but with his elbows raised sufficiently for him to be able to see through a cleft in the rocks, Thornton peered into the dimness, pushing his sight through the grey light of dawn, searching with eyes and ears for the slightest movement, the faintest sound that would give away the position of the hidden gunman.

Then a sudden movement right at the very edge of his vision. Cody! The other was crawling away through the rocks, moving slowly, dragging a foot behind him. Evidently his bullet had hit the other in the knee, smashing the kneecap and making it impossible for the other to put any weight on that leg. He drew his lips back in a tight grin. Slowly, he raised the Colt. This time, there was going to be no warning shout before he fired. Lifting the Colt, he fired quickly, ripping off four shots at the crawling man. He saw Cody jerk as the slugs hit him, saw him slump forward on to his face, his arms outflung, his injured leg drawn up at a curious angle under him.

Still Thornton did not trust the other. Easing himself forward gently around the smooth turn of the rocky overhang, he walked forward, the barrel of the gun tilted down to cover the other. But Cody did not move as he came up to him and he saw the ugly splotches of red that struck through the back of his shirt, showing clearly against the pale blue of the cloth. Turning him over with his boot, he stared down at the dead face and the wide open eyes before letting the other fall back into the dirt.

There was still Elton to take care of, he told himself. For a moment, he hesitated. It was not in him to kill his fellow men like this. Then he hardened his resolve. Just do it. Do it now and get it the hell over with. He looked about him, getting his bearings on this side of the trail, then moved in the direction where he knew Elton to be. Thirty yards, forty. He felt the tension beginning to crowd in on him. Elton was here someplace and he was still alive, although hit.

Then Thornton could hear him. There came the sharp scrape of a boot on the rocks, the metallic sound of a gun hitting something hard and unyielding. In his mind's eye, he could visualize Elton lying there, knowing perhaps that his companion was dead, that retribution was moving in on him among the rocks and he could not hope to get away. This time, even though there had been the two of them and they had figured their task was going to be so goddamned easy, they had soon discovered that they had caught a rattler by the tail and there was no safe way they would let it go without it biting them.

Bending, Thornton picked up a rock, threw it back-handed in the direction he had heard the round. There was an instant spurt of orange flame in the shadow between two of the rocks and the bullet whined off a boulder some distance away.

'Too bad,' he called derisively. 'I wasn't there.'

Another gunshot. This time the bullet broke rock a couple of feet away, but it was evident that Elton was still firing blindly. Thornton bent and waited. Two shots gone, but it was impossible to guess how many he had left. There had been plenty of time in which the gunman had been able to reload. He hurled another stone, but this time there was no answering shot. Elton was not taking any more chances.

Thornton decided to forestall any move the other might have in mind. The ground ahead was in his favour. Wriggling forward, then cutting sharply to one side, he entered a stretch of cactus-studded ground where he could move unseen into the gulch that curved away behind Elton's position. After a few minutes of scrambling over rough, stony ground, he came up among the rocks that overlooked the ledge on which the spread-eagled form of the killer lay. Elton was lying on his stomach, propping himself up on one elbow, his head turning sharply from one side to the other. There was blood on his shirt where Thornton's bullet had hit him in the side and his face was a pale blur. The faint jangle of a bit chain told Thornton where the other's horse was, a few feet away among the rocks. He smiled grimly to himself as he realized that although the animal was so close, Elton had been unable to summon up sufficient strength to reach it. Now he was doomed. Lifting himself slowly, squatting on his haunches on the smooth surface of the rock, he said softly: 'Here, Elton!'

Down below the other squirmed at the sound of his voice, flopped on to his side, jerking up his gun. Thornton's gun spoke once and the other fell back on to the rocks with a bullet in his heart.

CHAPTER FOUR

TWIN FORKS

Miles Thornton rode into Twin Forks shortly before ten o'clock. He tied his mount in front of the saloon and started for the steps, walking slowly and with the stiffness of long days in the saddle. He was hungry and felt the taste for beer to wash away some of the trail dust from his throat. Checking on Jeb Caldwell and Joe Fordham could wait for another few minutes. Besides, he told himself, here in the saloon was probably the best place to get the information he needed to find them.

At this early hour of the morning, the saloon was virtually deserted. A couple of trail hands sat at one of the tables and there were four more talking earnestly among themselves at another. The barkeep eyed him with a faint lift of his brows as he came forward.

'What'll it be, mister?' he asked, eyeing the trail dust on Thornton's jacket.

'Beer,' Miles said. He leaned his weight on his elbows, glad of the chance to relax.

The beer came a moment later and the bartender stood watching him as he drank it slowly.

'I was wonderin' if I might get a bite to eat here,' Miles

said, glancing at the other over the rim of the glass.

For a moment, the other hesitated, then shrugged. 'You can take your luck with what's left,' he said shortly. 'It's a little late for anythin' fine. If you ain't particular I can rustle you up some lamb stew.'

'All right, the stew will do fine,' Thornton nodded. He finished his beer, set the glass down on the counter as the other moved away, disappeared through a door behind the counter.

Two minutes later, the other came back, motioned him through into the kitchen at the back of the place. There were a couple of tables there, one bearing the remains of an earlier meal, the other set with a plate and eating utensils.

A stout woman stood over the stove in one corner, gave him a quick glance as he walked in and seated himself at the table. The smell of hot stew brought a sharp hunger pain to the corners of his mouth. He had ridden hard and fast since that brush with two of Clayton's men, not sure whether they were the only ones on his trail. He had seen no more during the last twenty-four hours and felt reasonably confident that none had followed him into Twin Forks.

The plate was heaped with stew and the woman brought him salt and bread, set them down in front of him, then moved back to the stove. The bartender stood in the doorway, watching him with a vaguely curious expression on his broad, fleshy features.

'You seem to have been ridin' hard and long, mister,' he said finally. 'Ain't often we get strangers ridin' into Twin Forks. You on business or just ridin' through?'

'I'm lookin' for a man,' Miles said. Out of the corner of his eye, he saw the other stiffen abruptly, knew what the man was obviously thinking and went on quickly. 'Ain't nothin' like that. He's a friend of mine. Last I heard he was here in Twin Forks, but that was some weeks ago. He could've ridden on since then and it's mighty important that I find him as soon as possible.'

'What's his name?' inquired the other. 'Could be that if he's still hereabouts, I'll know him. Most of the men come into the saloon at some time or another.'

'Nevin. Bob Nevin,' said Miles quietly. 'Young fella. Cowboy like me.'

The other considered that for a moment and then shook his head. 'Don't recollect any *hombre* by that name,' he remarked. 'We had a fella ride in about two – three weeks ago. Reckon he could've been the man you're lookin' for.'

'He still here?'

'Nope. Stayed for a day or so, then rode out. Headed west, I think. Most likely he was out for vengeance.'

'Vengeance?' Miles had been pushing the stew on to his bread. Now he looked up quickly at the other, scanning the man's face, trying to see something there which might tell him what the other had meant by that remark.

'This *hombre* rode into town, started askin' for two fellas, Caldwell and Fordham who had a spread a little way out from here west of Twin Forks.'

'Those were two of his friends,' Miles said quietly. 'This must've been Nevin.'

'Anyways, we had to tell him that both of these men had been shot down by a killer caller Duffield. He was foreman for the Bar X spread at Benson.'

The woman brought him a cup of steaming hot coffee. Miles felt her gaze on him, then she had moved back and the bartender was continuing his story.

'Weren't no doubt that Duffield murdered these two men. Neither was a gunslick and they didn't have a chance in hell against him, even though he goaded them into drawin' first, just to make it look legal.'

'So the law couldn't hold him here?'

'That's right. Duffield got off scot free. Claimed he shot in self-defence, that there were two of them against him.

Not that he needed to have done that. The sheriff we got here ain't too particular about the way he decides whether the law has been broken or not. The Bar X spread is the biggest and most powerful in these parts. If they were to decide to brace this town, there wouldn't be much of it left standin'. So Duffield got a warnin' and was let go.'

'And Nevin was told this when he rode in askin, for Caldwell and Fordham?'

'That's it,' agreed the other. The bartender hesitated. studying Miles face. 'You're figurin' that he rode into Benson to call out Duffield?'

'It begins to shape up that way,' nodded Thornton. 'If Nevin ain't in these parts, I reckon that I may find him around Benson.'

He dabbed his bread into the rich gravy until the plate was wiped clean, then sat back and rolled himself a cigarette. He felt better with food inside him and the stiffness was leaving his limbs. He debated whether to ride on to Benson at once, or make a few further enquiries around Twin Forks, finally deciding on the latter. There was no sense in going off half cocked.

'Better watch your step it you decide to ride on into Benson,' warned the barkeep. He leaned against the other table, surveying Miles closely. 'It's one hell of a town. Plenty of gunslicks there, most of 'em ridin' for the Bar X. If you try to set yourself up against them, you'll regret it. They're big and they're mean. We see a few of 'em in Twin Forks, but mostly they stick to their own backyard. Duffield was about the only one used to ride out as far as this for his fun.'

'This *hombre* Duffield sounds like quite a character,' Miles said steadily.

'He's as dangerous as a rattler, or a bull on the prod,' muttered the other.

Miles nodded. Inwardly, he wondered what may have happened if Bob Nevin had caught up with Duffield in

Benson. Once he heard about the slaying of his two friends, nothing would stop Bob from avenging them. That could either mean that Nevin was already dead, or he had been taken by the Bar X crew. Whatever had happened, things did not look too bright for Bob Nevin.

He paid the bartender, went out into the bright sunlight. The breakfast had stimulated him and he paused for a moment, then dropped the stub of his cigarette into the dirt, ground it in with his heel and made his way over to the sheriff's office on the far side of the street. The man seated behind the desk gave him an all-appraising look, then got slowly to his feet. 'Somethin' I can do for you?' he asked civilly.

'You the sheriff?' Miles asked. He gave the other an embracing glance as the man shook his head.

'Sheriff's out of town right now,' he remarked. 'I'm the deputy.' He motioned to the chair in front of the desk. 'Sit down and take the weight off your feet. From your appearance I can see you've been ridin, most of the night.'

'Thanks.' Miles accepted the chair but shook his head at the other's offer of a cigar.

The deputy leaned back and appraised him closely, as if he were searching in his mind, behind the mask of friendliness, for a face on some Wanted poster in the sheriff's desk. 'Now, what's on your mind?'

'I'm lookin' for a man called Nevin. I hear from the saloon that he may have ridden into town a couple of weeks ago. Seems there was a bit of trouble with a couple of his friends, fellas named Caldwell and Fordham.'

'Were they friends of his?' The other lifted his brows a little. 'They got into a fight with Charlie Duffield. He's the foreman of the Bar X spread. A real tough customer and fast with a gun, lightning fast – as they found out to their cost.'

'There was also some talk that this *hombre* Duffield

deliberately forced them to draw against him, knowin' he could outshoot 'em any time.'

The other's eyes narrowed at that and his brows drew together into a hard, straight line. 'Somebody seems to have been shootin' off their mouths,' he said harshly, 'or you heard wrong, mister. It was a fair fight and neither of those men needed to have drawn if they didn't want to.'

Miles shrugged. 'It was no concern of mine how it happened,' he said evenly. 'Just that if Nevin did ride in here and found that out, sure as anythin' he'd go gunnin' for Duffield.'

There was a significant pause during which the other continued to stare at him closely as though trying to make up his mind about him. Then the deputy gave a quick shrug of his shoulders. 'Whatever happened, it would be in Benson and that's outside our territory. I suggest that you ride on over there if you want to find out for yourself. Sorry I can't help you any further.'

Thornton waited for a moment, then got to his feet. He had the feeling that the other was deliberately holding something back from him, but he knew better than to try to push the other into talking. If there was something more, these lawmen would be particularly close-mouthed about it. He remembered how the other had instantly resented his suggestion that Duffield might have had a motive in forcing Caldwell and Fordham to draw on him. Nobody, clearly, was going to start bucking the dreaded Bar X crew, not even the men who were supposed to be upholding the law around here.

He went out of the door, stood on the edge of the board-walk for a long moment, leaning his weight against the wooden upright, contemplating the street in front of him, the harsh glare of the sunlight making the buildings stand out squat and square in every direction. They had clearly never been built for any other purpose than to be entirely functional, he thought. There was no beauty about this town, no curved lines on which to rest the eyes. The street itself was a river of dry dust that reflected back some of the harsh morning sunlight, hurting to the eyes.

On the point of moving down into the street and across to where his horse was tethered to the hitching rail, he paused as someone sidled up to him and said in a low, almost whining, tone: 'Heard you was looking for Bob Nevin, mister.'

Turning, Miles glanced down into the bearded face of the man who stood beside him. The other watched him out of beady eyes that held a hint of malicious humour.

'You know somethin' about him?' he enquired.

'Maybe.' The other nodded his head jerkily several times. 'But it's thirsty work talkin' and sometimes things get fuzzy in my mind. Not that I forget 'em, mind you, but—'

Miles was smiling. 'All right, I'll stand you a drink.' he said. 'Come along.'

Inside the saloon, they found a table away trom the door and Miles waited with a sense of growing impatience while the other tossed down the whiskey in front of him, took hold of the bottle and poured himself out another. Miles waited until that one had gone down, then said in a low, harsh tone. 'You were goin' to tell me about Bob Nevin.'

'Eh? Oh sure – Nevin. Why'd you want him?' The eyes took on their sly, beady look again.

'Never mind that. Just let it be enough to say that I've got to find him – and fast. There's somethin' happened that he has to know.'

'He's in Benson.'

'How can you be so sure?'

'I've just ridden in from there. Duffield was shot down in the street, less than a week ago. Whoever did it, and they all say it was Nevin, shot him in the back, never gave him a chance to go for his gun.'

'That's a lie!' Miles said harshly. 'Bob Nevin never shot a man in the back in his life.'

Involuntarily, his right hand had gone out, gripping the other tightly around the wrist. The old man tried to draw back, his face reflecting a little of the fear he felt at the look on Miles's features. With an effort, Thornton forced himself to relax.

'Sorry, guess I let my thoughts run away with me. Just that I know Bob Nevin, I've known him for a long time. He ain't the sort of man to shoot another in the back and I don't like to hear anybody say he did.'

The other nodded, poured a third glass, spilling a little on top of the table. He took a drink, set the half-empty glass down and wiped his sleeve over his mouth. 'I saw somethin' of what happened. Duffield had one of his men holed up in an alley to take Nevin from behind, like he always does when he ain't sure of the qualities of the man he's up against. Seems that somebody warned your friend about this, because he knocked this dry-gulcher out cold and then stepped out to call Duffield.'

He finished the rest of his whiskey. 'Nobody knows for sure what happened after that. There was a shot fired and then Nevin fired, but he reckons that there was some other *hombre* in the shadows, somebody who shot Duffield in the back and that he fired at this bushwhacker.'

Miles tightened his lips. 'Where is Bob Nevin now?'

'They've got him locked up in jail. But if I know the way the Bar X boys operate, he won't be there for long. They'll bust that jail wide open and string him up from the nearest tree.'

This was something that Miles had not figured. But it added to the urgency of the situation as he saw it. If Bob Nevin was to get back in time to help his kin, then he would have to be broken out of that jail – and fast. Pushing back his chair, he got to his feet, stood for a moment looking down at the old man. Then he gave a quick nod, strode to the door and went out into the sun-burned street. A couple of men sauntered by him, gave him a curious look as he walked quickly towards his horse, untied the reins and swung himself up into the saddle. He had hoped that there might have been a chance to rest up in Twin Forks for the day and continue the search for Bob Nevin the next day, but this news made that impossible now. At a rapid canter, he rode out of the town, not once looking behind him, pulled the brim of his hat down to shade his eyes against the blinding glare of the sun, lowered his head a little and climbed up the rocky trail that led out of the town, heading west.

He soon reached a flat stretch of ground and set his horse at a swift run, eyes on the trail in front of him, watchful for boulders and gopher holes that could throw his mount, break its leg and leave him stranded here. The hot wind blew in his face and the sun lay heavy and oppressive on his back and shoulders. The sunlight, reflected from the metal bits of saddle and bridle flashed painfully in his eyes and the heat rose swiftly as the sun began to lift towards its zenith. He was high up now, and by turning his head, could see for a long distance in the sun-hazed territory. Out to the south was a sea of desert, flat and featureless as far as the eye could see, all the way out to the sun-shimmering horizon that shook and shivered in the heat as if he were looking at it through a layer of wind-ruffled water.

Thornton was five miles out of Twin Forks when he felt the hills begin to crowd in on the trail from both sides, shoving their humped shoulders towards the road. Thin creeks ran down the steep slopes from the crests of the hills, blended into wider streams and finally joined into a wide, sluggish river that wound its way across the ground to the north. There was a narrow, rugged pass high in the upper reaches and he drifted towards it with caution, peering ahead of him into the sun haze. He did not know whether he was expecting danger, or whether it was a natural caution that made him move slowly; but as he came in through the pass, he observed the cluster of wooden buildings, set a short distance back from the edge of the trail, a little higher than he was.

Hesitating, he reined up, stared at the shacks through narrowed eyes. Then he switched his gaze a little, made out the gaunt yellow scars of old mine workings against the sheer side of the hill. Nearby, he noticed the scaffolding of wooden erections which had fallen into decay over the years.

When he reached the edge of the trail alongside the nearest of the buildings, he let his gaze wander over the ghost town, then drew in a sharp breath. He had seen several deserted ghost-towns such as this, but never one with smoke coming out of the chimneys. He did not doubt that this was a place for dodgers, men on the run, keeping one jump ahead of the law, with the smell of smoke and powder still clinging to them, forcing them off the trail into out-of-the-way places like this.

It was difficult to know if he had been seen already. Men such as these would keep look-outs posted to watch for the law, yet it was odd that they should be here so close to a main trail. He would have expected them to be further into the hills. Gigging his mount, he rode on for a little way, was halfway down the slope when a shot rang out from the boulders. The slug hummed past his head and ricochetted off one of the rocks. He swung instantly in the saddle, his right hand striking down for the Colt at his waist, then froze as a sharp voice commanded: 'Don't make a try for that gun, mister. If I'd wanted to kill you, that first bullet would have been in your heart.'

With an effort, Miles forced himself to relax, lifted his hands slowly to shoulder level, glancing out of the corner of his eye at the man who rose up from behind one of the rocks less than thirty feet away, the Winchester in his hands pointed directly at him.

'Turn around,' ordered the other harshly. 'Don't try anythin'. If you do, you'll regret it.'

'What is this?' Miles asked, forcing evenness into his tone. 'A hold-up?'

'Nope. Just wanted to get a good look at you.' The other stepped forward and Miles saw with a faint sense of surprise that he was an older man than he had reckoned, perhaps in his early fifties, his hair greying a little, an open tanned face disclaiming any pretence at being a man on the run. Miles furrowed his forehead in sudden thought.

'Can I put my hands down now?' he asked.

'Just so long as you don't do anythin' foolish,' nodded the other. The rifle barrel did not waver by so much as an inch. 'You a Bar X man?'

'No.' Miles shook his head. 'I'm ridin' through from Twin Forks.'

'Headin' for Benson?'

'That's right.'

'What you want there? Thinkin' of signin' on for the Bar X?' There was an odd edge to the other's tone.

Miles shrugged, guessed that he would not lose by telling the truth. 'I'm looking for a man. Bob Nevin. I heard back in Twin Forks that he's bein' held in jail on a trumped up charge of murder.'

'What's this *hombre* to you?' enquired the other. The tense expression on his face had relaxed a little.

'His father asked me to find him, and fast. There's big trouble back at his home and he figured that the boy might know what to do about it. Seems I'm a little too late '

The other regarded him closely for a long moment, then nodded to himself as though satisfied. 'Nevin didn't kill Duffield, the Bar X foreman, though he was spreadin' the word round Benson that he'd ridden in to do just that.

65

Maybe that's why they put him in jail.'

'The fella I spoke to in Twin Forks seemed to think that it was some other man who shot Duffield, somebody hidin' in the shadows of the boardwalk.'

The other nodded. 'Reckon he may have been right, at that.' he said enigmatically. He made a movement with the rifle. 'Now get off your horse and come with me.'

Miles made to protest, then realized that resistance would be useless in the face of the Winchester. Besides, warned a little voice at the back of his mind, there could be other men with rifles watching from the nearby shacks. Shrugging, he got down, led his horse up into the rocks, keeping a tight hold of the bridle.

When he reached the side of a two-storey building, the outer walls bulging precariously, the other motioned him to halt. Without turning his head. the man called sharply: 'Matt! Out here!'

There was a scrape inside the building and a moment later, a tall, dark-haired man came out, glanced at Miles from beneath lowered lids.

'Found him on the trail, Matt,' said his captor. 'Claims he's a friend of that *hombre* Nevin, they got locked away in the jail in Benson.'

'How do we know that?' asked the tall man, fixing his glance directly on Miles.

The other shrugged. 'Guess you don't,' he said, 'and I don't have any way of provin' it right now. Bob Nevin could prove it if I could get to him.' He had the odd feeling that he was speaking up for his own life here.

Matt scrutinized him closely for a moment, his face hard, then he said: 'Damned if I don't believe you.' He seemed a little relieved. 'But you ain't got a chance bustin' him out of that jail alone. You'll need help to do that.'

For a moment, Miles stared at the other in stunned surprise. 'You offerin' to help me?' he asked. 'But why should you do that?'

'One reason could be that we want to see the end of the Bar X spread. They've driven us off our homesteads and ranches, forced us out at the point of a gun, killin' and rustlin'. Now we've got to hole up here like rats, like hunted men, knowing that if we show our faces again in the valley, we'll be marked men, a target for any Bar X killer who spots us.'

'Any other reason?' Miles had the unshakable feeling that there was something more he ought to know.

The other paused, then nodded his head. 'One more,' he affirmed. 'I'm the man who shot Charlie Duffield in the back that night just over a week ago. It ain't easy to sleep at night knowin' that another man is goin' to be strung up for somethin' you did yourself.'

'I get it now,' Miles said. 'But how many men do you have? Enough to ride openly into Benson and get Bob Nevin out?'

'There are ten of us here. Not enough to tackle the Bar X crew openly, even with Duffield dead. But there may be a way of getting your friend out of jail.'

'Tonight?' Miles asked.

The other considered that, then gave a brisk nod. 'I guess so. You can rest up here until it gets dark, then be ready to ride out with us. I figure that we owe Nevin this much anyway.'

There was a bunk in the lower room of the house and Miles stretched himself out gratefully on it. There was a deep-seated weariness in his bones and limbs and it was difficult to recall when he had last slept well. Relaxing, he closed his eyes and was asleep almost at once.

He had dozed for perhaps six hours when he was wakened by a touch on his shoulder, bringing him wide awake at once. There was still a faint glimmering of daylight left, but it was fading swiftly in the west, where the sun had gone down behind the low hills, leaving them black and purple against the skyline, while the red-fired sunset lay in all its glory beyond them.

Matt stood over him. He said quietly. 'Time to be movin' out. The boys are all saddled up and ready to move. Tonight we teach the Bar X crew that they can't kill our neighbours, burn our homes, and get away with it for all time This time, we're goin' out to put matters right.'

Turning on his heel, he went back outside and Miles got slowly to his feet, buckled on the heavy gunbelt, checked the cylinders of the Colts, then thrust them back into leather, straightening up a little. He felt refreshed after the sleep and his mind was alert again.

Outside, his mount was ready. The rest of the men were already in the saddle, grim, silent men, who sat with the last red rays of the setting sun on their faces, etching them with shadow. He swung himself up into the saddle, threw one last look about him at the gaunt remains of the buildings, then followed the others along the narrow, dimly seen rocky trail.

CHAPTER FIVE

BREAKOUT

At times during the week, Bob Nevin would think of the man who had been killed by an unknown assassin, trying to figure out why anybody should have shot Charlie Duffield in the back and then slunk off into the shadows leaving him to take the blame for it. During that time, he had found for himself that Will Rowland was a straight and honest man, but he knew also that the sheriff was coming under tremendous outside pressures to have him turned over to the Bar X crew who had their own method of meting out justice. Nevin knew that he would get short thrift once those killers got their hands on him.

Most of the time though, Nevin stood at the cell window, staring out through the bars into the street below him, trying not to think of anything. The murders of Caldwell and Fordham had been avenged, but not in the way he would have wanted. He had tried to do the honourable thing, call out Duffield on even terms, but fate had decreed otherwise.

Blinking his eyes in the dimness, he had watched the sun go down over the hills to the west, had heard the bunch of riders come into town and seen them as vague shadows when they had made their way over to the saloon. Very soon afterwards, there had been the usual brawling, the drunken yelling and singing, the tinny piano being played by the man brought specially from way back east for the job, to keep the customers amused and happy between games of poker and faro.

But this evening, as the minutes had slipped by into hours, it had come to him that there was something more to the singing than on other nights. There was an undercurrent of menace abroad in the town that night, something he could feel, sense. He wasn't sure what it was, except that it boded ill for somebody, and he had the unshakable feeling that he was the focus of that hatred.

Going over to the door he pressed the side of his face as close to it as possible, and tried to make out the sounds from the outer office. Will Rowland had brought him his supper a little while before and now the empty mug and plate were on the floor just inside the door, waiting for the other to come back and collect them. Even as he stood there, the interconnecting door opened, and a pale shaft of light illuminated the passage. Rowland came along it, paused outside the door, then said harshly.

'All right, Nevin, pass the plate and mug to me.'

Bob bent to do as he was told, handed the utensils through to the other and as Rowland made to turn away said quietly, 'There's somethin' afoot in town tonight, ain't there, Sheriff? Trouble brewin'.'

'What makes you think that?' asked the other sharply. He paused, turned to contemplate Nevin through the bars.

'Just a feelin' I've got in my bones. Saw that bunch ride in a little while ago and head for the saloon. Some of the Bar X crew, I suppose?'

'They could've been,' admitted the other. 'But so far they've given no sign that they mean trouble. They've been in town most nights this week and we've had it real peaceable.'

'But it won't be like that tonight. You're as jumpy as I am Sheriff. I can see it in your face. You're expectin' that mob to head for the jail any minute and force you to set me free so they can take me out and string me up. That's it, ain't it?'

'You're talkin' foolish,' muttered the other. He tried hard to make his tone sound convincing, but only partly succeeded. There was a strained note of worry edging every word and his voice was pitched a shade too high for perfect ease.

'All right, Sheriff. So you reckon I'm wrong. But at least, if they do come and try to bust me out to lynch me, I've got a right to defend myself.'

The other narrowed his eyes at that. He said: 'If you're figurin' on me handin' you a loaded gun, then you're loco. The law says that you're my prisoner until the circuit judge gets here to hold a hearin'. That's how I intend to keep it.'

Bob shook his head slowly. 'You reckon that you can hold off that mob if they really get themselves likkered up and decide to get me out? You know damned well you can't. Not even if you swore in half the town as deputies. Nobody would face up to those trained killers just to save my neck from a rope.'

'You still stickin' to that story of yours?'

'Nothin' else I can do. It happens to be the truth, whether you like it or not.'

'I must admit you don't look like the type of man who'd shoot another in the back,' replied the other, 'but I've learned never to go by appearances. They can be dangerously deceptive.'

'You checked on that dry-gulcher who was in the shadows?'

'No.'

'Why not?' Bob demanded. 'Even if you figure I'm lyin', the least you could do is check out my story. Whoever it was on the boardwalk, he sure enough wanted Duffield dead,

71

just as much as I did, because that slug wasn't aimed for me. I was at least twenty feet from Duffield when that shot was fired and they say it hit him plumb centre in the back.'

Rowland furrowed his forehead in sudden thought. 'Yeah,' he admitted slowly; 'that's right, it did. I hadn't figured it that way before. The few folk who saw the shootin' say that Duffield was in the street facin' you when he was shot so it couldn't have been your slug that killed him unless it ricochetted off the boardwalk.'

'You reckon that's likely, Sheriff?'

'Maybe not. But right now, I can't do anythin' but hold you here, no matter what I might think in the matter. This will all come out at the hearin' as soon as the judge gets here.'

Bitterly, Bob said: 'You think I'll still be alive by then? From the sound of that mob out there in the saloon, somebody is gettin' them pretty well likkered up, ready for action.'

Rowland backed away from the door. His face was taut and grim. 'I reckon I know how to handle these *hombres*,' he said solemnly. 'I've got a bunch of my men over. They'll stay with me in the office through the night, or until that bunch of men ride out.'

Without another word, he strode off along the passage and a few moments later, Nevin heard the metallic clang of the door shutting. Darkness lay in the passage and he turned back into the cell. Going over to the window, he peered out into the dimly-lit street. It was almost completely dark now, although a few yellow lights cut into the street from the windows of the buildings on either side. He caught glimpses of one of the deputies as the man walked along the far boardwalk, carrying a rifle in his hands, his face alternately lit and then shadowed. He doubted if these men would do much against the Bar X ruffians once they decided they had plucked up enough courage to storm the jail.

When it happened, he wondered how Rowland would solve his own conscience, or whether the other had a conscience when it came to something like this. It was an unenviable job these frontier lawmen took on and inevitably they had to be as hard and tough as the men they fought. Mistakes were made, innocent men hanged or shot, but slowly things were moving in the right direction, even though it would take time before complete law and order was brought to the west.

An hour passed. Still the noise came from the direction of the saloon. If anything, the men in there were becoming more and more rowdy. He could guess at what was happening. Whiskey giving them the courage to attack the jail. He was only surprised that they had not made the attempt earlier.

Lifting himself on his toes, he tried to see the saloon entrance, but it was too far along the street and his line of vision too restricted. He was on the point of going back to the bunk when the faint movement at the corner of his eye attracted his attention. Someone had slid from one shadow to another in the mouth of the narrow alley ten yards away. He stared directly at the spot but could see nobody. Had he imagined it? A trick of the light brought on by his over-wrought imagination?

The silence got on his nerves. It was just possible that the noise in the saloon was a cover for another group of men to move in on the rear of the jail and snatch him under the very noses of Rowland and his deputies. He felt a little shiver go through him and there was sweat lying on his body and forehead as he strained to push his sight through the clinging darkness around the mouth of the alley.

A moment later, a man drifted out of the deep night-shadow, paused for a moment, looking about him in both directions, then began to sidle along the boardwalk, moving in the direction of the jail. The faint yellow light from across the street glinted on the gun he carried in his hand. Behind him came another man, bent low, a lariat in his hands.

So that was their game, he thought grimly. He wondered whether to yell and warn Rowland and the others. There was the thin scrape of footsteps in the narrow back street that ran along the side of the jail. Less than ten seconds later, the leading man was just outside the cell window. a dark, formless blur of shadow.

'Bob! Bob Nevin?' called the other softly, urgently.

For a second, surprise rendered Nevin speechless. Was this a trap to get him to give away his position? As soon as he answered to his name, would a Colt be thrust in through the window, finishing him there and then?

'Bob! For God's sake if you're in there answer me. This is Miles Thornton.'

'Miles?' Reaching up, Bob gripped the bars of the cell window with fingers that tightened convulsively around the hard, cold metal. 'What are you doin' here? How did you manage to find me?'

'Never mind that now. We've got to get you out of there while that crowd are still whoopin' it up in the saloon. There too many of 'em for us to handle. At least in a straight fight.'

'The sheriff and a bunch of deputies are in the outer office.' Bob warned.

'Yeah, we figured that. We've been watchin' them for close on half an hour now. We'll try and pull the bars out of the window. They don't look too secure to me.'

A second later, the other man had sidled up to the wall. The lariat was looped securely through the bars, then led across the street to where a third man had brought one of the horses. Fastening the other end of the riata to the saddlehorn, the other paused for a moment, then slapped the animal hard across the rump. The rope tautened as the animal strained. Bob stood a short distance from the window, watching as the rope held. He could make out the bars bending a little under the tremendous strain, but they still held. For perhaps twenty seconds, the silent duel continued. Then, with a tremendous ripping sound, the whole metal frame came loose from the window, tearing some of the stone with it, sending it crashing down into the street and leaving a wide, ragged gap in the wall.

'Quick, Bob!' urged Miles harshly from the shadows outside. 'Let's get the hell out of here before that brings them all running.'

Scrambling forward, ignoring the rough stone that tore at his fingers and the backs of his hands, Bob pulled himself through the hole. Hands reached in and grabbed at him and a moment later, he was through, standing in the narrow street. The racket from the saloon seemed to have drowned out the noise they had made and Miles caught at his arm, urging him along the alley, out to the main street.

'We've got the horses along here.' he said through tightly clenched teeth as they ran. 'That mob in the saloon aren't goin' to hold off for much longer. They seem to be on the point of movin' right now.'

Reaching the horses, they swung up into the saddle. As he caught hold of the reins, Miles thrust a Colt into Bob's hand. 'Better take this,' he said tersely. 'You may need it before we get away from here.'

Even as he spoke, the doors of the saloon behind them opened, and a flood of men came down the wooden steps into the main street, began to surge in the direction of the jail. Turning his head, Bob saw them move in a body to the front of the jailhouse, heard the harsh yelling as they paused there. He reckoned there were close on thirty men in the bunch. Men in an angry mood, ready for anything.

Bob walked his mount slowly along the street. By now, they were beyond any of the buildings with lights in the windows and the shadows lay thick and huge on the street.

With all of the yelling and raucous shouting behind them, it seemed possible they were going to make it out of town before they were seen, but this was not destined to be the case. A man standing on the edge of the crowd outside the sheriff's office turned his head, saw them, yelled a harsh warning: 'There they go. Somebody must've busted Nevin out of jail.'

'After them!' shouted another voice. 'Don't let them get away! We want Nevin alive if we can get him.'

Bob wheeled in his saddle, sent a couple of shots bucketing along the street and saw one of the men clutch at his chest, stagger and then go down, crumpling into the dusty street. The others scattered and began to come on at a slow run, moving along both sides of the street.

Miles called out. 'Leave them be, Bob. Get out of here before they get their horses.'

It made sense. Sooner or later, the men would go for their mounts, most of them tethered in front of the saloon. While they were on foot, there was little to fear from them. Stray shots followed as they gigged their mounts, raking spurs along their flanks, sending them at a run through the main street and out into the open country to the south of Benson, where the trail curved away across the flat prairie. There was no moon and they were forced to ride in the complete darkness with only the tall clumps of pine, standing up from the flatness on either side of them, standing out against the skyline. Bob was not too sure of where they were headed but he trusted the men who were riding with Miles. Where the other had picked up these men and how he had found out where he was, he did not know as yet. But for the time being, their main concern was to put as much distance between themselves and the Bar X men as possible before dawn.

For almost half an hour there was no sign of any pursuit. Then, as they rode up a steep rise, they reined up their mounts and glanced behind them and Nevin was just able to pick out the faint bunch of flickering lights far back down the trail.

'There,' said the tall man who rode close beside him, the man he had heard Miles call Matt. 'They're carryin' torches to see the trail. At least we can keep them in sight which is more than they can do as far as we are concerned.'

'Don't be too sure of that,' Miles said quietly. 'It could be a trap to lull us into a state of false security. That may be only part of their bunch, carrying those torches so that we figure we know exactly where they are, but in the meantime the rest of the bunch are circling around to the west or east, coming up on us in the dark. If they are, then they could be on us before we know it.'

'He's right,' Bob said crisply. 'It's just too obvious. We'd better ride and keep movin' until dawn when we can see 'em clearly.'

'What about the rest of you boys, Matt?' Miles asked, turning to the big man. 'You've done what you set out to do, helped me get Bob here free. Are you ridin' back now, or comin' with us?'

'Guess we'll ride with you,' said the other after a brief pause. 'We got nothin' here until the Bar X is finished, and I doubt if we can do that alone.' He looked at Bob as he spoke. 'Your friend tells me you've got troubles of your own. Could be that we can be of some help.'

Bob looked puzzled for a moment, then turned to Miles. The other said quietly: 'I'll explain things to you as we ride, Bob. But like Matt says, we can do with every gun we can get. There's big trouble back at the spread. The mining company is movin' in on everybody, hounding 'em off the range, shootin' and rustlin'. Many of the smaller men are on the edge of bankruptcy and others have been forced to sell out at rock-bottom prices. All hell is goin' to break loose there, believe me.'

77

'Then I guess we'll be glad of your help, Matt,' Bob said. He threw one last quick glance at the advancing men behind them, then kicked rowels at his mount's flanks, urging it on at a rapid run.

Fifteen miles further on, they ran into a dense thicket. It stretched all the way across the trail, which wound in and out in a manner which forced them to slow their pace to a walk. Even then, the low snake-like branches whipped over their faces, slashing at their flesh, threatening to blind them every second. Bob's face was numbed and bleeding by the time they eventually came out of the thicket, located the trail once more and rode on into the night. At least, the thicket might help to throw their pursuers off their trail. He wondered just how far those men of the Bar X would follow them.

Dawn greyed the eastern horizon and found them climbing slowly into the hills. They passed through one belt of timber, tall growth pine that lifted sheer to the heavens, the thick canopy of leaves blotting out the dawn for a long moment, until they came out into the open again, into more rocky, rugged ground that lifted even more steeply.

They paused on one of the narrow ledges and looked back at the trail they had followed through the night. The grey light softened the harsh contours of the low foothills, but as far as they were able to see the trail was empty. There was no cloud of slowly drifting dust to indicate the presence of a bunch of hard-riding men spurring after them. He let his breath go through his mouth.

'I figure we've thrown them off the trail,' he said quietly. 'Reckon we can rest here for a while. I'd like to know what's been happenin' back home, Miles. Why you had to come after me in such a goddamned hurry.'

They dismounted, led their horses into a narrow opening off the ledge, found the shallow creek that came rushing down through a channel of smoothly-shaped rocks and stones cut in the side of the cliff. Bob went down on to his hands and knees, drank his fill of the cold, clear water, then wiped his face and neck with it, before sitting up and glancing across at Thornton.

'All right, Miles,' he said finally. 'What is all this about?'

The other rubbed his chin, the scrape of his fingers on the stubble loud in the stillness. 'It started nearly a year back, I reckon,' he said softly. 'The Mining Corporation sent a handful of surveyors on to the territory. They started measurin' up the place, puttin' up markers on the range. They didn't seem to care where they went, whether they was trespassin' or not. Finally, they was run out by some of the ranchers. About a month later, a fella called Vergil Clayton rode into town, set up an office there and let it be known that the mining company had the deeds to all of the territory around there. Said that the court had backed them up and they intended to take over. They reckoned that the deeds that any of the ranchers held were illegal, meant no more than the paper they was written on.

'That was when your father and the others decided they weren't goin' to be run off their land, that they'd stay and fight. But Clayton brought in a bunch of hard-cases, men fast with their guns. Cattle started bein' rustled, men shot from ambush. Only the day before I rode out, three of the boys had been caught on the edge of the ranch. One was shot dead, the other two were strung up from one of the cottonwoods. We brung their bodies back to the ranch and it was then that we saw Clayton and some of his men ridin' in. I figure they came to give one last warnin' to your Dad, Bob. He told me to hit leather and find you, tell you what was happenin'. He said you might be the only one to help us now.'

'But those land deeds that the ranchers have were granted by the Government in Washington shortly after the war finished,' Bob said tightly. 'They're all perfectly legal.

Why didn't the ranchers take the case to one of the big courts out East?'

'You think that they hadn't figured that before? Trouble is that Clayton has got most of the trails watched. He'll stop anybody who tries to get through. Nobody has a chance.'

'And if all of the ranchers banded their forces together?'

'Wouldn't do any good, Bob. They don't have as many men as Clayton can lay his hands on, and all of his hired men are gunslicks, seasoned killers. Our men don't have much chance against critters like that.'

Bob nodded, rubbed his chin thoughtfully. He had never dreamed that things could have been as bad as this. At the moment he saw no way out of it, but to stand and fight. He knew now why Miles had asked Matt and the others to ride with them, what he had meant when he had said they would need every gun they could get to back them. There was a growing tightness in his mind as he sat there, staring off into the stunted trees, where the brightening dawn was just beginning to touch them with a faint red flush.

Making a cigarette, he lit it and drew on it slowly. Maybe if he could round up all of the men that Clayton had turned out or had rustled their cattle, they would be able to fight the mining company's gunmen then with the help of the men riding with him now.

'You got any ideas, Bob?' Miles asked, glancing at him sharply.

'Nothin' definite,' he admitted. 'Just tryin' to figure how many men we can call on, countin' Matt there with his men.'

Miles pursed his lips. 'Hard to be sure You may have an evenly matched force as far as men go, but when it comes to pitting a cowpuncher against a hardened gunman there can be only one end.'

'I know. But it's the only chance we've got.' Bob finished his cigarette, tossed the stub into the racing water of the creek, got to his feet and moved over to his waiting mount. They still had a long distance to cover and now the rising urgency which had gripped Miles during his search for Bob, had transferred itself to him. There was no way of telling what Clayton would be doing while he was away.

The morning brightened as the sun rose and they made their way along the steep switchback courses that led up through the hills which barred their path. With the passing of the long morning the heat grew more intense and several times they were forced to slow as they encountered fresh dirt slides on the narrow trail, necessitating edging their way forward an inch at a time, knowing that one false move by man or horse could send them plummeting over the lip of the sheer-sided precipice to certain death on the rocks a couple of hundred feet below.

It was, as Bob well knew, a dangerous trail. But now time was precious and every minute they could save could prove to be vital. This route was the quickest there was to the ranch, could lop four hours off their journey.

The afternoon passed slowly. Bob could feel the urgency boiling up inside him, blotting out all other emotions in his mind. It was difficult to think straight with this thrusting at his thoughts as he rode, his eyes flicking now from one side of the trail to the other, watchful and alert for trouble. Before dark they would be on the edge of the territory which the mining company had marked for its own, and he tried to figure things out logically in his mind, thinking ahead as much as possible, assessing the probabilities as he knew them, rejecting one idea after another in his attempt to find a solution to the problem that faced him.

It wanted an hour to dusk when they rode round a curve in the trail and came down out of the hills, hitting the flat stretch of ground which would eventually give way to the lush green grass of the plains that bordered the valley on which the Circle Four ranch had been built. There were no signs of trouble until they rode into a narrow valley with the smooth-sided hills drawing close on to the trail from both sides. At the end of the valley, as Bob remembered, lay the Killearn ranch; just a small place, a long, low-roofed log cabin, a small corral and a barn. Here lived old Jeb Killearn, his wife and his son Ben. Bob sought in his mind, realized that Ben would be almost twenty now. It was difficult to imagine him as grown up, maybe as big as he was.

They rode slowly out of the valley, with Bob in the lead and Miles just behind him. Bob glanced about him, ready to call out to the Killearns who they were, just in case the old man had a rifle on them and was feeling edgy with all of the trouble that was threatening to break in the territory. Then he pulled up his mount with a sharp tug on the reins. There was no sign of the cabin, or the barn. Only a pile of ashes and the twisted beams of the buildings were visible.

Nevin sucked in a sharp gust of air, then urged his mount forward until he reached the burnt-out shell of the ranch-house. Dismounting, he walked forward, his feet stirring up the grey-black ash which lay everywhere. There was the sharp smell of burnt wood still hanging in the air but he guessed that this had happened some days before, maybe weeks.

Miles walked forward beside him, then turned to stare at him, his face a pale grey blur in the dimness. 'Looks like Clayton's work,' he said dully.

Bob nodded numbly. 'You any idea when this happened, Miles?'

Thornton shook his head. 'I'd heard nothin' about it when I rode out lookin' for you. Must've been since then. It's pretty clear now that Clayton meant every word he said. He threatened that those who didn't accept his offer to get out peacefully, would be burned out. I wonder what happened to the old man and his family.'

'Either shot or made to leave before the place was razed.'

Bob felt a wave of savage rage rush through him and his fingers clenched so tightly by his sides that the nails dug deeply into the palms of his hands, but the anger was so great that he scarcely felt the pain. 'They'd have no chance against Clayton's gunmen.'

'Now you can see for yourself what we're up against,' Miles said tightly. 'And you'll see why it's not goin' to be easy to get these folk to back you against Clayton. When they know that he can strike at any time and without warnin', they don't like the idea of tryin' to stand up to him. They'd sooner try to cut their losses and get out with whole skins.'

'There must be some of them who'll stay and fight if they see an even chance of winnin',' Bob said thinly. 'If they all run, then Clayton will take over, whether it's legal or not. And once that happens, nobody will get their land back, because the courts will simply decide that there's no sense in reversing the situation, especially if it's goin' to lead to further bloodshed. The authorities won't want a full scale range war on their hands if they can do anythin' to prevent it even if it means that all of the small ranchers are goin' to be done out of their livelihoods.'

Grimly, Miles said: 'Whether they want a full scale range war or not, if your father has his way, that's exactly what they're goin' to get. He's a stubborn man, Bob, as you probably know.'

CHAPTER SIX

BURN-OUT

From the window of his office, Vergil Clayton stared moodily into the bright sunlight that slanted into the street outside. His hands were clasped tightly behind his back and he had stood in this pose for almost two minutes and the man standing near the desk was beginning to feel more and more uncomfortable as he waited for Clayton to speak.

Finally, the other said harshly: 'You're sure you recognized him when he rode into the Circle Four ranch? There was no mistake?'

'None at all, Mister Clayton. I know Bob Nevin by sight and that sure was him. He came in last night with Miles Thornton, one of the Circle Four hands and a bunch of riders. I didn't recognize any of them, but he sure looked like he meant business.'

'This could mean that I may have to alter my plans a little,' affirmed the other harshly. He turned away from contemplation of the street, went back to the desk and lowered himself into the red plush chair behind it, stretching out his legs in front of him, his forehead creased with lines of concentration. 'I can't risk sendin' all of the boys out to the Circle Four now, to take care of old Ben Nevin. Those could have been gunmen that came in with his son.

It's too much of a gamble at the moment and I'm not a man used to takin' unnecessary risks. There are other ways of finishin' off the Nevin family than tryin' to burn them out.'

He took a cigar from his top pocket, bit the end off and spat it on to the floor, then thrust the cigar into his mouth and applied a match to the end, sucking on it to light it. Blowing smoke out in front of his face he spoke through it. 'If the other ranchers get the chance to side up with the Nevins, they could make it difficult for me, even with the men I've got. I'll have to go about this slower and easier than I figured.'

'I figure we could take 'em without too much trouble, if we was to hit 'em right now, before they're ready for us.'

'Maybe so. But I don't aim to take that chance, not when there's another way to go about it. Remember a week or so back, they were all set to talk themselves into bandin' together and attackin' me. Then we burned out the Killearns and that pretty soon put a stop to any ideas they may have had. I reckon that's the way we have to go about it from now on. We'll take 'em one at a time, burn 'em out, shoot anybody who tries to resist. By the time I'm finished, there won't be anybody in the territory who'll care to stand with the Nevins against me.' He brought his huge fist crashing down on top of the desk to add emphasis to his words.

'Where do we start this time?' asked the other.

'I figure we ought to pay a little social call on the Dawneys. Sam Dawney has been shootin' off his mouth in town ever since the Killearns were hit, spreadin' it around that I was responsible. So far, nobody seems to have taken much notice of him, but I don't intend to let this go on much longer. Another reason too. Dawney has a daughter, doesn't he?'

'That's right,' nodded the other. 'June Dawney. Nice lookin' gal too.'

'So I hear. I also hear that Bob Nevin was fond of her when he was here a few years ago. Things may have cooled off between the two of 'em since then, but I figure there may still be some of the old feelings left and if we hit the Dawneys, it'll be a fine warnin' to Bob Nevin to stay out of my way.'

The other man looked dubious. He rubbed his chin thoughtfully, then traced a line with a horny fingernail down the side of his nose. 'It could also make Bob Nevin real mad. That might not be wise.'

Clayton shook his head and there was a leering, vicious grin on his face as he looked up from his desk. 'Anger makes a man do rash and stupid things, Clem,' he said meaningly. 'It could work that way for Nevin too. If he comes ridin' for me without thinkin' things out, all the better for me. That way, he'll be playin' right into my hands.'

Clem grinned. 'I reckon I get the picture,' he said harshly. 'When do we head for the Dawney place?'

'Get half a dozen of the boys together and ride out after dark tonight. I guess we've got no reason for delayin' it.'

'Sure.' The other went out and Clayton sat back in his chair, smoking his cigar, watching the slanting beams of sunlight where they struck through the dust and smoke in the room. He was beginning to feel a little better now that he had made up his mind what to do and saw good hope of success. When he had first heard of Bob Nevin's arrival at the Circle Four with a bunch of gunmen, the news had come as a complete surprise to him. He knew then that it had been Thornton he had spotted riding hell for leather from the Circle Four spread that night when he had ridden in to try to force Ben Nevin's hand. Evidently the other had been ordered to head out and look for young Nevin, to bring him back before trouble really broke in earnest.

He pondered that thought for a long moment, felt a faint edge of fear in his mind. If that was the case, then it meant that Cody and Elton had failed in their mission, which had been to overhaul Thornton and finish him before he could bring help. He knew now, with a feeling of certainty in his mind that both Cody and Elton were dead. Clearly Thornton was a man to be reckoned with, along with Bob Nevin himself, who had built up quite a reputation for himself along the frontier as a man deadly fast with a gun. Finishing his cigar, he got to his feet, went out of the office, locking the door behind him. He made his way to the sheriff's office, went in without knocking. Hester, the sheriff, was a big man, his face the colour of beet, with the veins standing out on his cheeks and nose, eyes too close together for good looks. He looked up angrily, opened his mouth to snap a sharp retort, then simmered down as he saw who it was, forced a broad smile that twitched his lips but never reached his eyes.

'Oh, it's you Mister Clayton,' he said fawningly. 'Somethin' I can do for you?' He waved a hand towards the other chair.

Clayton shrugged, lowered himself into it and regarded the other from beneath lowered brows. 'I want to know exactly where the law stands regardin' those land deeds the ranchers hereabouts reckon they've got.'

For a moment, a glitter of surprise showed in Hester's eyes, then he lowered his lids, shutting it out. 'I reckon you know that as well as I do. Your claims are recognized by the law, in town. You reckon there might be any trouble?'

'There's already been trouble as you well know, Hester,' Clayton said tonelessly. 'None of these ranchers are goin' to move out peaceably. That's why I've had to hire me these gunsharps to enforce the law. Seems I'm gettin' very little backin' from the town.'

Hester spread his hands on top of the desk in a futile gesture. 'I've tried to make my position clear,' he said slowly, choosing his words deliberately. 'I'd bring a posse to back your men, but in this town—' He shrugged and let his voice trail away into an apologetic silence.

'I know what you're tryin' to say,' Clayton said fiercely. He leaned forward in his chair, fingers holding the sides with a white-knuckled grip. 'The town is backin' these men who're intent on defyin' me. You couldn't call together a posse to ride out and back me, even if you wanted to.'

'Now that ain't quite right, Clayton,' Hester protested. 'It's just that these ranchers have been here for a good many years now, and the townsfolk have got to look on them as friends. Ain't likely they'll go against these men now, just on my say-so.'

'Yet if the positions were reversed, and you were askin' them to stand up against me, they'd come willin' enough.'

'I didn't say that.' Hester shook his head emphatically. 'I got no control over the men I deputize, until they've been sworn in. Even then it ain't easy to get them out in a bunch. You don't think it's easy orderin' them to die for what you think to be right, or ride out and fire the homes of these folk.'

'And if I do decide to fire these ranchers to teach them a lesson? What then? You reckon you can hold the townsfolk if they decide to take the law into their own hands?'

'I guess so.'

'Guesswork is no good to me, Hester,' Clayton snapped harshly. 'I want to know exactly where I stand with these folk in town. I don't like to think that I might be stabbed in the back just when I'm least expectin' it.'

'There won't be anythin' like that, I promise you,' said the other thickly. He looked uneasy, sitting upright in his chair.

'I only hope for your sake that you can stand by that promise,' Clayton said getting to his feet. 'Because now that Bob Nevin has ridden into the Circle Four with a bunch of gunmen, I'm havin' to take matters into my own hands. If you ain't with me in this, then you'd better see to it that you're not against me. Because I'm goin' to win this battle and when I do, I shall remember all of this.'

'I get your point,' said Hester sullenly. 'There won't be any trouble from the townsfolk.'

'Good.' Clayton gave a brief nod. 'See to it they don' get in my way and there won't be any trouble as far as the town is concerned. I don't want to have to be rough on them but I guess you know what can happen if a bunch of hot-headed ramrods decide to brace a trail town of this size.' He could see by the look in the lawman's eyes that his words had got home.

It was early evening, and Bob Nevin glanced up at the darkening sky and wondered if events were developing. He had half expected Clayton to make some move during the past day, but so far there had been no indications that the other intended doing anything. Maybe, Bob ruminated, somebody had seen him ride back into the ranch with these men and had guessed that he was there, ready for a showdown. If that was the case, and word had somehow got back to Clayton, it might have been sufficient to give the other pause, forcing him to alter some plans he had already made.

Ben Nevin came out on to the porch, threw a quick look at the sky, then crossed over the courtyard to where Bob was standing. 'There's somethin' about to happen, Bob,' he said softly. 'I can feel it in my bones.'

'Clayton?'

'I figure so. He's not the type of man to sit still and do nothin'. If he knows you're here, ready for trouble, he'll strike before we get a chance to defend ourselves.'

Bob nodded. He remained silent for a moment, then said: 'I was thinkin' of taking a ride over to the Dawney place tonight. Just to see if I can persuade them to throw in their lot with us. They must've heard about the Killearns by now and if they don't make up their minds pretty quick, they won't be around to fight.'

Ben Nevin regarded his son closely for a long moment. Then he nodded in understanding. 'You still thinkin' about June Dawney? She's grown up a lot since you were last here. Maybe she won't remember you.'

Bob smiled. 'Maybe not. But it won't take long to bring

back her memory. She was a regular little spitfire in those days. I wonder if she's tamed down at all since then.'

'I guess there's only the one way for you to find out.' The older man gave a quick nod. 'But be careful. Clayton has his men everywhere. They watch every trail, ready to shoot first and ask questions later.'

'I'll keep my eyes open.' Bob whistled up his horse from the corral, threw on the saddle, bent to tighten the cinch, then mounted up, checked the Winchester in the boot and his two Colts before gigging his mount forward, across the courtyard and past the bunkhouse. Miles Thornton was standing in the open doorway. He called out softly: 'Want me to ride with you, Bob?'

'No, this is a chore I can do myself.'

He set his horse to the hill trail, circled the edge of the spread at that point, then passed through the gate in the perimeter wire and made his way through the tall timber to the crest of the hill. At the top, he paused, looked back along the trail he had come. He could just make out the yellow lights which shone from the windows of the main building, the shadowy shapes of the horses in the corral and it came to him that from where he sat, it made an excellent target for anybody intent on hitting the place and taking the men there by surprise.

His fears were lessened a couple of minutes later, when a tall shadowy figure rose up from behind a clump of rocks, the long-barrelled Winchester levelled on him. He started abruptly in the saddle, saw the other man lean forward a little and then the rifle was lowered as the man said: 'Oh, it's you, Bob. Figured it might be when I spotted you headin' out along this trail into the timber.'

'You keepin' watch here through the night?' Bob asked.

The other nodded, set the butt of the gun down on the rock and leaned on it for a moment. 'That's right. You never can tell if Clayton will decide to send come of his boys this way.'

'Well watch your finger on that trigger if you see a lone-some rider headin' back,' Bob said, with a faint grin. 'It's likely to be me.'

'I'll watch for you,' said the other.

Bob rode on, glanced back a moment later, before he reached the bend in the trail, but there was no sign of the man. He had gone down out of sight among the rocks.

At the same time that Bob Nevin set out from the Circle Four, Clem Tassard and fifteen of Clayton's men rode over the brow of the low rise that looked down on the Dawney spread, reined their mounts on the low hill and sat hunkered forward in their saddles, waiting for Tassard to give the signal to ride down. They had ridden hard from town, covering ten miles in less than half an hour and there was still a faint glow in the west where the last vestiges of daylight were clinging tenaciously to the heavens as though reluctant to give pride of place to the approaching night.

'How many did you say were down there?' growled one of the men harshly.

'Three or four men and the girl,' Tassard answered. 'There's to be no shooting unless they decide to make a fight of it. If they come out with their hands lifted when I yell, then we herd them out of there and fire the buildings, put 'em into one of the wagons and see them on their way.'

'Those other folk decided to make a fight of it.'

'These people may.' Tassard's voice suggested that it was a matter of complete indifference to him what the Dawneys did. If they surrendered and did as they were told, it would make things a little easier all round, but if not, then there would still be no problem. He could not see the few hands down there standing up to the men he had behind him, men thirsting for a gunfight. 'Spread out now and surround the place. Whatever happens, I don't want any of them gettin' away and warnin' any of the other ranchers.

91

Leastways, not until we've got them all in one of the wagons and away from here.'

The gunhawks moved their mounts off, slowly and silently, moving through the dusk with a grim purpose as they took up their positions around the small cluster of buildings. Tassard waited until he judged they were all in position, then moved his mount forward a little way, cupped his hands and called loudly: 'You in there, Dawney?'

There was silence for several seconds, then a voice came back from one of the windows at the front of the building. 'I'm here. Who's that and what do you want at this time of day?'

'This is Clem Tassard. I've got men surroundin' you. Come out here, all of you and with your hands lifted, and there'll be no trouble. Try to resist and it'll mean the end of all of you.'

There was a further pause and he guessed that the other was holding a hurried council of war with the rest of his crew. Tassard waited while the silence piled up, then called again. 'I'm goin' to give you a minute in which to make your minds up. If you ain't out at the end of that time, we're comin' in shootin'.'

'You're the same bunch of killers that attacked the Killearn place, ain't you?' There was no fear in the voice that came back out of the darkness. 'You're paid by Vergil Clayton to kill and plunder. Well this is your answer and it's the only one you're goin' to get.'

A split second later, the night was blown asunder by the sharp reports of rifle fire and the spitting orange flames from the windows were clearly visible a moment before the lead began humming around Tassard. He slid instinctively from the saddle, but not before a slug had burned his upper arm, robbing it of all feeling.

Cursing loudly, he stumbled into the rocks that surrounded the place, yelling harshly to the men to pour their fire into the buildings. Bullets screamed in from all sides to smash the windows, splintering the glass into fragments. The echo of the shots merged swiftly into an almost continuous roll of thunder as it was thrown back and magnified by the surrounding hills. Tassard lowered his rifle and lifted his head slightly to observe the effect of the rifle fire. There were still the bright stilettos of flame showing from most of the windows. Slugs were striking the rocks very close to his position and a second later, the man lying next to him suddenly uttered a low, throaty moan and fell over on to his side, his rifle slipping from his grasp and clattering down among the rocks.

Savagely, he pulled up his own weapon, levered another shell into the breech, gritting his teeth as pain lanced redly along his arm. It was all he could do to keep the rifle steady, even though he leaned the barrel on one of the rocks in front of him, sighting it on one of the smashed windows, waiting for a face to show itself. But the defenders were keeping themselves well down except when they lifted their heads for a quick shot into the darkness.

Blue gunsmoke rose on the still air and Tassard moved over the dead body of the man lying beside him, as he headed for the cover of another low rock formation a couple of yards away, crouching low as flying lead hammered the ground around him. Two other men had been hit and were lying behind the rocks, firing desultory shots at the ranch buildings. He muttered harshly under his breath as he realized that things were not going at all as he had expected. There must be more men down there with Dawney than he had imagined. But with a complete circle of his men around the place, there could be no possible escape for anyone in there. Thirty yards now separated him from the front of the ranch and a split second later, he saw the face which appeared at the window, fired a snap shot and saw it vanish. It was impossible to tell whether his shot had gone home but he had the feeling that it had.

For the best part of fifteen minutes, the firing continued, now fading a little as the men were forced to reload, now burgeoning up again in renewed violence. At length, Tassard leaned back on his good arm and yelled: 'All right, Dawney, you've asked for it. Get the torches ready men. We'll burn them out!'

He lay there, waiting while the men brought the torches they had carried on their saddles. Once they were lit and flaring in the darkness, he called out harshly: 'This is your last chance, Dawney. Ain't no sense in stayin' there and havin' your place burned down about yours ears while you're still in it. You've got that daughter of yours to think of. You wouldn't want her burned to death, would you?'

'I'd prefer that to the sort of justice that you coyotes deal out,' called a rich feminine voice. 'I've heard what happened to the Killearns. But sooner or later, somebody is goin' to catch up with you and then you'll all be swinging on the end of a rope, with your legs kicking at the air.'

Tassard hesitated for a moment, flushing at the girl's words. Then he cried: 'All right men. Go in and burn the place!'

Nevin had crossed the wider trail which swung around from town and intersected the main stage trail some ten miles further west and was now less than two miles from the Dawney ranch. The horse frequently slowed, tired from the long ride out from Benson and knowing its own mind, not responding too well to his urging. He watched the grey-black foreground of the trail where it wound like a faintly-seen scar over the landscape and felt the tension in him heighten as he smelled dust hanging in the air, indicating other travellers close by.

Ten minutes ride brought him to a narrowed section of the trail, where rocky walls crowded in on him from both sides, the track so narrow in places that his legs were scraped against the rock as he rode through. He was just heading out of the canyon when he caught the unmistakable break of gunfire from directly ahead of him. For a moment he paused, listening to it, judging its direction and intensity. The firing stayed long and brisk, surging, swelling volleys that told of a large number of men. Then it died away a little except for sporadic shots potting each other at frequent intervals. In spite of the tension in him, he drove the horse forward at a rapid trot, keeping the point of the rowels hard against the animal's heaving flanks, ignoring its desire to slow and pick its own pace.

Jumping forward into a dispirited run, it carried him over the rough, rugged wasteground that fronted the boundary of the small spread. A ragged burst of shots rang out and then, as he came through a stand of dry timber, he caught sight of the pulsing orange glow in the near distance, saw the flickering of flames. The sight spurred him on, heedless of the danger from the ragged, upthrusting rocks which dotted the trail at this point. Everything was quite clear to him now. Clayton had struck at the Dawney place, taking advantage of the darkness to take the others by surprise.

No sooner had he come in sight of the ranch than he dismounted on the run, ran for the cover of the rocks and crouched down, holding tightly to the Winchester which he had grabbed from the boot. Narrowing his eyes, he could just make out the shapes of the running men advancing on the ranch-house. The small barn had already been set on fire and the flames were leaping a score or more feet into the still air, a shower of sparks travelling in the direction of the ranch itself. Gunfire still came from the ranch and even as he crouched there he saw two of the attackers, bearing their flaming torches aloft, stagger and fall on the edge of the courtyard, crashing on to their faces in the dust.

Swiftly, Bob glanced about him, looking for signs of the other men he guessed were hidden among the rocks.

Whoever was leading these killers would not have sent all of his men in to burn the buildings down. He would have kept some of them back to give covering fire to the others.

A moment later, he saw two of the men lying behind the low boulders less than twenty yards away, immediately below him. They were lying flat on their stomachs pumping shot after methodical shot into the windows of the ranch. The red glow from the blazing barn now provided them with sufficient light by which to pick out the individual windows, while they themselves remained in dark shadow. It was an almost ideal offensive position for them.

Lifting the rifle, he laid the sight on the nearer of the two men, took up the slack of the trigger, paused for just a moment, aware of what he was about to do, to shoot a man in the back without any warning. He would then be nothing more than a dry-gulcher. The thought lasted only a few seconds in his mind. Then he told himself that June Dawney was somewhere down there, was maybe wounded or dead already. That thought was clear enough for him. He tightened his finger a little more and the rifle bucked against his wrists. He saw the dark shape of the man jerk, stiffen, then roll sideways out of sight among the rocks. The second man got to his knees, lifted his head and stared about him fearfully, striving to make out where the shot had come from. It must have been obvious to him how impossible it would have been for any of the men in the ranch to have fired that shot. He was turning to stare directly in Bob's direction, when the other sent a slug into the man's chest, pitching him back against the boulder, where he hung in an attitude of crucifixion for a long moment before his legs gave under him and he slid down on to his back to lie still.

Running sideways to a fresh position, Bob sent more slugs crashing down among the gunmen. At the moment, he was not striving to kill more of them, rather he wanted to put confusion into their minds, to make them believe they had been hit by a large force, taking them from the rear. The shimmering starlight gave him all the light he needed to make out the prone figures of the men among the rocks and for those nearer the ranch-house, the glow from the burning barn gave more than adequate light. He threw a swift glance in the direction of the house and noticed with a sense of relief that the defenders were still keeping up a regular fusillade of shots against their attackers and as yet the men with the torches had made little headway towards the house itself. At the moment, they were crouched down behind the horse troughs and piles of fodder around the outside of the yard, pinned down by the rapid and accurate fire.

A hoof turning on rock was his first intimation of the presence of a man close by, and he drew his Colt, snicking back the hammer softly as he steadied the weapon. Then he saw the faint shapes of the horses less than ten feet from where he was crouched and edged forward slowly, keeping his head well down, eyes alert. The man standing guard over them was obviously uneasy. He had picked out the sound of gunfire to his rear and knew that it portended another attack.

Drawing back his lips over his teeth, Bob moved to one side and brought up the gun sharply as the guard whirled, catching his movement at the very edge of his vision. The other's gun was already lifting to cover him when Bob squeezed off a single shot. The other jack-knifed violently as the heavy slug slammed him back against the rocks. His legs gave under him and the gun in his hand hammered once, the bullet spanging off the rocks.

Pulling his knife from his belt, Bob slashed at the long tie-rope which tethered the line of horses, then fired the gun twice in the air, spooking the animals. As they plunged down the slope, he heard a loud voice shouting from the direction of the ranch.

'Some jasper has set the horses loose. Get up there after him. Leave the Dawneys for the time bein'.'

97

Bob smiled grimly to himself. Now he really had got these critters worried. For the next five minutes, he was a fleeting, elusive shape, darting from one concealing shadow to another, firing at the gunmen whenever he saw them, adding to their confusion and uneasiness. In the small courtyard, the men with the torches had given up the attempt to fire the house and were pulling back, firing as they ran, dropping their torches into the dry dust where they fizzled out one by one. Shots from the windows of the ranch followed them into the darkness.

Sporadic shots came from the rocks and trees which bordered the small ranch. Answering flame came from Bob's guns and the rifles used to good effect by the defenders in the house. But gradually, the firing from the Clayton bunch faded as they pulled out, unsure of the strength of the opposition which faced them and increasingly aware of their own predicament now that their horses had been run off.

Bob grinned as the last shots died away, the echoes fading into the distance. Holstering his gun, he moved out to the edge of the courtyard, called loudly. 'You in there, Sam?'

There was a pause, then a voice yelled back 'I'm here. Who's that?'

'Bob Nevin. Heard the ruckus a while back and managed to throw a scare into those *hombres*. Mind if I come on in?'

'All right. But move in slow and keep your hands where I can see 'em. There are half a dozen rifles lined up on you.' There was no mistaking the grimness in the other's tone.

Keeping his arms well away from his sides, Bob strode briskly forward. It gave him a faintly queasy feeling in the bottom of his stomach, knowing that those guns were trained on him, that itchy fingers were on the triggers. It needed very little to set them firing again.

Ten feet from the front door, he halted. A moment later, the door opened and Sam Dawney appeared in the opening. He held his Winchester in his hands, pointed in Bob's direction, as he leaned forward a little, peering into the smoky, flame-shot darkness. Then he lowered the gun.

'By all that's holy, it is you, Bob,' he said, coming forward. He thrust out a hand, grasped the other's warmly. 'When did you get back?'

'Yesterday,' Bob said. He glanced over the other's shoulder in the direction of the barn. 'You'd better get some men into tryin' to put that fire out, Sam. Then we can talk. I figure there's a lot we've got to talk about.'

'You're durned right there is,' muttered the other. He turned, yelled an order. A few moments later, the rest of the men came out of the ranch-house, moved towards the barn, picking up buckets and filling them at the pump, tossing the water on to the flames, although from what Bob could see of the fire it had got too firm a hold for them to have any hope of putting it out before the barn was totally destroyed, but at least they could prevent the fire from spreading to the house itself.

Glancing back as another figure came out of the house, Bob found himself staring although he had not meant to do so. June Dawney came up to him and there was a faint smile on her face. Even in the flickering glow of the flames, he saw that she had indeed blossomed out into a beautiful woman. When he had last seen her she had been in pig-tails, a boyish figure.

'Hello, Bob,' she said warmly. 'It's been a long time.'

'Too long,' Bob said, 'and I'm only sorry that we had to meet under such circumstances.' Anxiously, he went on: 'But you're all right? You weren't hit in that shootin'?'

She shook her head and the rich chestnut curls danced on her shoulders. Her level gaze was fixed on his. 'One of the boys was hit, but that's all.' She looked at the barn and her mouth tightened. 'You seem to have come back only to ride into trouble. Vergil Clayton means to kill us all.'

CHAPTER SEVEN

THE WILD ONES

An hour later, the barn had burned itself to ashes and four men had been sent up into the timber to watch for any further attack, although Bob was doubtful if Clayton would try anything more that night after he had suffered such an ignominious defeat at the hands of a much smaller force. Not that it would dampen his determination to drive the ranchers off the range. But it might mean he would be forced to alter his plans a little more.

Wearily, Bob sank down into the chair in the small front parlour, stretched his legs out in front of him, and forced himself to relax. June came in with coffee and he sipped the hot liquid gratefully, feeling it bring some of the warmth back into his weary body.

'What do you figure on doin' now?' he asked, after a brief pause. 'I saw what happened to the Killearn place when we rode in.'

'They were hit a week or so ago,' Sam Dawney explained. 'Nobody knew about it until some days later, when they came through here in their wagon.'

Bob felt a wave of relief. 'Then they weren't killed in the attack?'

Sam shook his head. 'No. Clayton led his men out on that

100

attack, ordered them out of the house, told them to put what they needed on to the wagon and ride out. When they'd done that, he and his men fired the buildings. He said he didn't want any trouble, but they'd have to go as they were trespassing on the Mining Corporation's property. I got the same warnin' tonight, but I reckoned I'd fight.'

'But the next time he comes, he'll have more men with him and he won't give you a chance. He'll hit you without warnin'.'

'We've already had warnin',' declared the other harshly. 'They won't take us by surprise again.'

'No, but they may be far too strong for you the next time,' Bob said seriously. 'I hope you realize how dangerous it's goin' to be so long as Clayton is in power here and can throw his men against you. I've got a feelin' too that we can expect no help from the town as yet. You know anythin' about the sheriff they got there now?'

Sam Dawney's lips twisted into a sneer. 'Hester! He'll throw in with the party that pays the most and is most likely to win through in the end, and in his eyes, that's Clayton. Whatever you do, son, don't trust Hester an inch. He'll have some charge cooked up against you so he can toss you into the jail and so long as you're there, you won't be able to help us fight Clayton.'

Bob nodded. 'It only needs Hester to get word from Benson and he'll have all the ammunition he wants for arresting me.' he muttered grimly. He saw the faint quirk of surprise on the other's face, saw the girl watching him narrowly from near the doorway and explained quickly what happened in Benson, ending with the shooting of Charlie Duffield and the manner in which he had been broken out of jail so that he might ride south and help against Vergil Clayton.

Dawney waited until he had finished, then rubbed his chin thoughtfully. 'Like you say, son, that's all Hester will need to ride out here with a warrant for your arrest. And he'll sure get it. The judge in town is on Clayton's side, ain't no doubt about that. We've tried to get our deeds to these lands proved legal in the court there, but he's thrown out our papers every time. We even hired ourselves a fancy lawyer from back East, but he had no luck either. When you've got a crooked judge and sheriff, ain't nothin' you can do except take the law into your own hands and fight it out with a gun. I'm a peaceable man myself, but when it comes to some critter like Clayton and those he works for trying to force me off my land, then I ups and fights. Only thing to do.'

'I reckon that goes for everybody in the valley,' Bob said slowly.

'We know most of the odds that are stacked against us. But we've got everythin' to fight for, our homes, land, families and future. Those gunslingers who're ridin' with Clayton got only money, I reckon. Could be it's goin' to depend on who's got the best incentive to win this fight.'

Bob nodded, but remained silent. He had the feeling that there was a little more to it than that, but he did not want to make things appear any blacker than they were at the moment for fear that he scared these people off. If Clayton was to be defeated, they needed every man they could get to join in the fight against him.

They talked for a while longer, then Bob went through to the back room, to where a bed was ready for him. Taking off his clothes, he stretched himself out on it, revelling in the touch of the cool, clean sheets against his tired body. The night air blew cool through the smashed window where bullets had ploughed through the glass into the room and there were some signs of the damage which had been caused.

He thought about the men on guard around the ranch, knew that after what had happened during the early part of the night, none of them would sleep while on watch, but nevertheless, he put his gun under his pillow then turned over on to his side, turning things over in his mind, for although there was a deep-seated weariness in his body, his mind was still active, throwing up a host of questions which he found difficult, if not impossible to answer. The position, as he saw it now, was fairly clear. This Mining Corporation had somehow discovered that there were valuable mineral deposits on this land. Probably those surveyors who had come into the territory, ostensibly to size up the place, had been geologists, looking for minerals and their report had made the company suddenly aware of the fact that there were riches to be had here in the territory if they could only move in and claim the land for themselves. They could have bought everyone out, giving them a fair price for their land, but even if they had done this, Bob knew there would be several of the older diehards who would not sell. So the company had decided to take a different course of action. They had attempted to bluff the folk into believing that their claim to the land was based on worthless deeds which would not stand up in a court of law; and to back this up, they had made certain that the first cases to be heard in town had been decided in their favour.

Now they were intent on terrorising the ranchers and the small nesters into getting out, some selling their property for a pittance, a mere fraction of what it was worth. The others would be killed or run out of the territory and by the time they were able to get the original deeds declared legal, it would be too late, the Mining Corporation would be in full control.

Now that the first real seeds of resistance had been sown, and it had been shown that Clayton's men could be driven off if a determined stand was made, there was just the chance that the other ranchers would throw in their lot with them and stand against this tyranny which had appeared in the territory. Only if everyone backed them, though, would they have an even chance of defeating Clayton. By the time the Mining Corporation became aware that there was trouble here which Clayton and his band of gunhawks could not control, it would be too late for them to do anything about it.

He closed his eyes and tried to sleep, but the uneasiness in his mind made it difficult for him to relax. He could relax his body, but how did one relax the mind? As far as he was able to see, the only course open to him would be to shoot fast and straight at every Clayton rider and take every possible opportunity to whittle down the odds which were stacked so high against them. Ruthlessness was their best weapon now against a man such as this. Only that way could they ever hope to succeed.

The sun was well up when Bob finally woke, blinking his eyes against the sunlight that filtered into the room. He sat up quickly, dressed, shaved, then went down into the kitchen. He heard the clatter of pots and pans before he reached the door and opening it, found June getting the breakfast ready. She glanced round as he entered, gave him a quick smile.

'I thought it would be a shame to wake you early,' she said. 'There was no more trouble through the night and you looked as if you needed the rest.'

'It was a long ride out from Benson the other night,' he admitted. He let his gaze rest on her face, saw the faint flush which stained it a pale crimson. Then she lowered her glance, said softly: 'You've changed a lot since I last saw you, Bob. You seem to have grown more – self-reliant, more confident of yourself. I suppose that's only to be expected. I hear you've been a lot of places and seen a lot of things during the past few years.'

'That's true. And you, June, you've changed too. When I left, you were just a girl in pigtails, who was always so sure she could shoot faster and better than I could. Though I suspect that you cheated on several occasions.'

'Do you expect me to admit that?' she asked with a low laugh.

'No, I guess not. After what 1 saw last night, I reckon you must still be able to handle a rifle.'

'All I want is to see Vergil Clayton dead,' said the girl thinly. There was a determined glitter in her eyes. 'What do you think we ought to do, Bob?'

He was silent for a moment, then said softly: 'I think it might be best if you were to come over to our place, stay there until this is finished, one way or another. If everybody is scattered about as they are now, in little groups, Clayton's men could ride right over them, one at a time, before any help could get through to them. But if we're all together in the one place, we can face them on more even terms.'

She considered that for a moment, then nodded. 'You're right, I suppose. Have you put it to Dad?'

'No, I'll have a talk with him after breakfast. Then I want to ride into town. There's some business there I have to look into.'

He saw the faint look of alarm on the girl's face at that remark. 'Do you think it would be wise to go into town just now, Bob? Clayton will have you jailed, or killed.'

'He has to catch me first. But I want to have a talk with this judge who has been handin' down these decisions against the ranchers. If I can get evidence that Clayton has been payin' him for this, then it will go a long way towards gettin' them convicted if we can get word through to the federal authorities of what's goin' on here.'

'But the few men who tried to get through to warn the authorities of what is happening here were either turned back or killed.'

'That's true. But I figure that if we keep right on at Clayton, he'll soon have his hands so full that he won't have the men to watch all of the trails out of here and that's when we'll do it.'

The girl said nothing, but began to set the dishes on the table, then divided the bacon, eggs and bread out. There was a jug of hot coffee on the stove, the aroma filling the kitchen. Sam Dawney came in a few moments later, gave Bob a brief nod, seated himself at the table and motioned the other to do likewise. Bob guessed that the rest of the men were either eating in the bunkhouse, or were still up in the hills on watch, taking no chances.

Silence reigned while they ate, then when he had finished, Bob put his proposition to the older man. Sam Dawney listened until he had finished, then flicked a glance at the girl before saying: 'All I've got in the world is here, son. Reckon you know that. But there's a lot of truth in what you say. The only way that Clayton is goin' to defeat us is by takin' us one at a time. With a big group of men we may even be able to carry the attack to him.'

'That's what I'm hopin',' affirmed Bob. He sipped the scalding hot coffee. 'It's up to you and the others. Don't let me try to influence you either way. It may be that Clayton will decide not to try to take this place again, that he'll transfer his attentions elsewhere and you could come out of this with whole skins. On the other hand, he may be so mad at what happened, that he'll send all of his men tonight to overwhelm you and if he does, he'll leave no survivors, he'll give you no choice of livin' or dyin'.'

His words fell into a muffling silence and he could see by the looks on their faces that they understood every word he said. Finally, Sam Dawney said harshly: 'We'll pack everything we can and ride over to the Circle Four today, Bob. You'll be ridin' with us?'

'No, there's a chore I have to do in town and unfortunately it's one that won't wait.'

Before he could elaborate further, June burst in on him: 'He means to ride in and talk with the judge, Father. Can't you talk some sense into him? They'll kill him rather than let him ride out of town again.'

There was a perplexed look on the other's face. 'Is this

true, Bob?' he asked.

Bob nodded. 'I want to see if I can prove that the judge is in cahoots with Clayton and that crooked sheriff they've got in town. With that evidence in my hands, I think we can force Clayton's hand.'

'You may have changed somewhat in five years or so, son, but they'll still recognize you in town. If you're seen, it could be the end of you. You say that they may be able to hang somethin' on you from Benson way.'

'I don't intend to let anybody see me but the judge,' Bob said firmly. 'I still know my way around town. I figure I can get in there, and out again, without bein' spotted.'

'I hope you won't regret this decision,' Sam replied. 'It won't be easy to get near the judge. He's not an easy man to find when he's not in court.'

'I'll find him, never fear.' Bob got to his feet, pushing back his chair.

It was mid-afternoon when Bob Nevin rode from the small ranch and headed in the direction of town. The rancher and his daughter, with their hired hands, had pulled out half an hour earlier and Bob had watched as they had taken the trail out towards the rim of the Circle Four spread. He felt certain they would be as safe there as anywhere.

He rode slowly past the embers of the burnt-out barn, felt a sudden rise of anger deep within him, then forced it away as he set his mount to the steep trail that climbed up into the hills. He had deliberately waited until this hour of the day before leaving, so that it would be dark by the time he approached the town, thereby reducing the chances of being seen.

As he rode, he saw landmarks which evoked distant memories in his mind. In those far-off days, everything had seemed good. It was possible to ride through the whole of this territory without carrying a gun, or wondering what might lie behind the next bend or up in the rocks that over-looked the trail. Those were the good times, when the cattle grew fat and there was no smell of gunsmoke over the prairies. Maybe it was because he had been young, and the troubles of the world, whatever they may have been at the time, had little place in his life.

But would those days ever come again to this troubled valley? He had the unshakable feeling that before they did, there would be a time of violence and bloodshed, that men would die to bring it about. Dipping down from the hills, he skirted the main stage trail that wound over the desert towards Benson and rode parallel with it, but some distance away, keeping it in sight throughout the long, dusty afternoon, so that he might watch any travellers who might be on it, but during the whole of that time he saw nobody, no sign of any riders in the distance. By the very absence of any movement, the desert seemed to give an indication of things which were still to come and in spite of himself, he felt a tiny shiver move up his spine and there was a curious tightness in his chest which he had learned, from the past, never to ignore.

Timber intervened between himself and the trail and he lost sight of it for the best part of an hour before the trees thinned and the slope began to move down in the direction of the plain once more. Slowly, he traced his way back to the road as the sun began its long, downward dip to the western horizon, throwing long, dark shadows over the trail. The road was a solid streak of grey dust now, standing out against its background. As he rode, June Dawney's warning kept coming back to him, repeating itself over and over in his brain. 'Be careful of the town tonight.'

He thought of her more and more as he made his way along the narrow valley. There had been an intimate friend-ship between the two of them in the old days before he had ridden out, but now he was a little uncertain of how she felt about him. As for himself, he had felt a strange surprise at the way she had grown over the years. It seemed unlikely that five short years could have wrought such a change in anyone, yet in her case she had become a grown woman, with a woman's charms and the ability to pull a man with or against his will. It would be easy to love a woman like that, he thought to himself. But unless they were able to defeat this menace which had come to destroy them, there would be no chance for him.

He reached the town an hour before midnight and circled around it, scouting the place out before moving in. A few lights still showed in one or two of the buildings at either end of town as well as in the saloons and the hotel. The place seemed to have grown bigger since he remembered it. There were more buildings put up near the centre of the town where the two main streets intersected in a wide square but even in the darkness, he could see that the big cottonwood was still there and he guessed that the old circular wooden bench which ran all the way around the base of the trunk would be there also.

Satisfied finally, he rode slowly along one of the narrow alleys, came to a standstill outside a low-roofed shack that stood alone on a plot of ground filled to overflowing with piles of rubble and rubbish. If he were still alive after all these years, Bob knew that this shack belonged to Cant Fergus, an old prospector, shunned by most of the folk in the town, and a man who only used the place at infrequent intervals whenever he was in town to get more supplies and spend what little dust he got from panning the streams up in the hills on cheap rotgut whiskey.

As he had figured, the place was empty and there was the smell of dust in the air as he made his way inside, feeling around in the pitch blackness, after leaving his mount tethered to the rear of the building, out of sight of any prying eyes. Pulling down the wooden shutters on the two windows, he checked that no light came in before bringing out the small lamp and lighting it, setting it on the low table.

Evidently, he thought, glancing about him, it had been quite a while since Fergus had been to town. But there seemed little chance of him wandering in that time of night; and even if he did, Bob was quite sure that the other would not give him away. From what he remembered, Cant had little love for the law or the ordinary citizens of the town.

Sitting down in the creaking chair at the table, he considered his position. So far, no one here knew that he was in town. He turned over in his mind the most likely place where the judge would be at that time of night and eventually decided that if he was not at the hotel, where he usually put up when he was in town, he would be with Clayton in one of the saloons, or pow-wowing with the sheriff. There was also the judge's chambers near the end of the main street where he kept most of his legal papers. There would be files there and it was possible he could find some evidence of connivance there without getting hold of the judge himself.

He waited for twenty minutes or so, then swept his cupped hand over the top of the lamp, extinguishing it, and stepped to the door, checking up and down the alley before stepping out into the night. There was the sound of voices in the distance where the alley ran into the main street and, standing there, he saw the three shadows move past the opening and vanish. Evidently, he thought, the town was still awake, was likely to remain so for another two or three hours yet, until everybody got tired of drinking and went back to sleep it off.

He circled around the block on foot, not trusting his mount in all that stillness. When he finally came out into the main street again, he was further from the centre of it although he could still see the glare of yellow light from the saloon next to the Mercantile Store. He cast about him for a moment until he was certain it was safe to go out, then strode catfooted along the boardwalk, eyes flicking from side to side, watchful and alert for trouble.

There was the feel of danger on all sides of him, and that

curious little itch between his shoulder blades, so that he caught himself hunching his neck and shoulders forward, tensing himself. He thought: 'What use is a shoulder against a .45 slug?' and somehow forced himself to relax as he made his way forward in the pitch darkness on this side of town.

The small office stood a little apart from the buildings on either side of it, in a plot of ground, weed-covered now, with a couple of stunted trees growing on either side of the narrow path that ran up to the front door. Bob paused in the shadows for a long moment, contemplating the situation, letting his gaze rove in all directions before making a move. When he did go forward, he deliberately moved around to the rear of the building, found a window, the glass covered with a layer of dust and inserted the blade of his knife against the catch. A swift twist and he heard the snap of the rusted lock.

It was not in him to wait. He had come too far and had hunted too long to pause now. Thrusting the window open, he clambered inside. The musty smell of the place came to him, assailing his nostrils as he edged forward, listening intently. Something scrabbled across the floor, skittered into one of the unlit corners. The gritty sound faded as the rat vanished and that was the only sound he heard as he moved away from the window.

He recalled that he had once been in this place when old Judge Hendreys had been alive, but that had been many years ago and he doubted if he could recall the whereabouts of anything now. He did not dare to light a lamp and knew he would have to find his way around by sense of touch.

Setting one foot slowly in front of the other, easing his weight down quiet and smoothly, he crossed the room, fumbled for the door on the other side, found the handle and opened it carefully. Beyond lay darkness. Listening, he heard nothing, but there was an uneasy coolness ruffling the small hairs on the back of his neck. Going through the doorway, he found a partition in front of him and once he had

111

made his way around it, he found a dim greyness in front of him where a faint light was reflected into the front room through the window that faced on to the street. It was dim, but sufficient for him to see objects by. There were two windows looking out over the patch of rough ground towards the street and he padded forward until he reached one of them and, pressing himself hard against the wall to one side, he peered through the curtainless window into the darkness.

The street in the distance appeared to be totally deserted as far as his limited field of vision allowed him to see, but a moment later, he heard the run of a horse in the distance, a ragged, dispirited run of an animal, tired and weary, being pushed hard. Seconds later, he saw the rider go by at a rapid trot. In the darkness, the distance had been too far for him to recognize the man but whoever it had been, the other was in a hurry to reach his destination. Maybe, Bob reflected, it had been one of Vergil Clayton's men riding in with the news that the ranchers were gathering.

He dismissed the other from his mind, looking around for the wooden shutters, found them placed neatly against the wall in one corner and fitted them into place over the windows. Not until this had been done did he light the hurricane lamp and place it on the floor where there would be little chance of any chinks of light showing through cracks in the shutters, but he would have sufficient light to see by.

There was a low, roll-top desk against one side of the room and he went over to it, checked all of the drawers. One containing a few scraps of paper was open, but a quick glance through told him there was nothing of importance there. The other three drawers were locked. Again the impatience in his mind overrode any qualms he may have had about breaking into this place and he forced the locks with the long-bladed knife. There were several legal documents there, stacked in neat piles and in one of the drawers a small derringer pistol, loaded and cocked ready for use.

He debated whether to remove it, then decided against it and let the weapon lie where he had found it.

Seating himself at the desk, he scanned through the papers. Most of them concerned cases which the judge had heard in the town court but there was nothing to connect with any illegal connivery with Vergil Clayton and the mining company. Baffled, Bob thrust them all back and got slowly to his feet. Maybe he had been looking in the wrong place all the time. It had been a relatively easy matter to force the locks on the desk drawers; and no doubt the judge would have realized that too and seen to it that anything incriminating would be in a really safe place.

A safe! Bob looked to his left and right, discovered nothing, but he knew there had to be a safe somewhere, probably in a corner of the room or maybe one of these newfangled things built into the wall. He moved slowly along one wall, feeling carefully with his fingertips. Then, at the far corner, he paused. A sudden sound reached him from outside the building. Swiftly, he moved to the lamp, extinguished it, placed it back on top of the desk, and edged away into the rear room.

The sound of horses stopped outside and there was the distinct jingle of a bridle in the ensuing stillness. Then he heard the faint crush of footsteps on the path outside the door and a moment later, the soft murmur of voices. Slowly, he pulled the Colt from its holster, gripped it tightly in his right hand, and waited. A key turned in the lock of the door and a second later, it was pushed open. Peering through the crack in the door in front of him, he made out the two shadowy figures who stood there, pausing on the threshold as if unsure of themselves.

One of the men had a gun in his hand, and as he moved forward, a glitter of metal showed on his shirt. The sheriff and the judge, Bob thought tightly.

'Reckon Slim could've been mistaken, Judge,' said the

sheriff harshly. 'It ain't hard to imagine a light in these buildings and he said himself he was ridin' pretty fast.'

'No, somebody has been here.' The other's tone was sharp. 'Those shutters on the windows. They've been put there. I left them stacked in the corner.'

'Why would anybody want to break in here?'

'That's what I intend to find out.' The two men moved into the room, the judge closing the door behind him. Lighting a match, he lit the lamp and set it on the desk, peering about him in the yellow light. To the sheriff, he said tersely: 'Reckon you'd better check that rear room, just in case.'

Bob saw the lawman nod, move in the direction of the half-open door. Before the other could reach it, he stepped out and paced forward into the room, his gun covering the two men.

'Just drop that gun, sheriff, and you judge, raise your hands and you won't get hurt.' He prodded the lawman in the side, saw the other wince as the gun barrel bored into his flesh. For a second, the thought of action lived in Hester's eyes, then he reluctantly released his hold on the gun, letting it fall with a thud to the floor. The judge's hands had already shot up towards the ceiling, but there was a shrewd, scheming expression on his face as he stared across at Bob.

'Who are you, mister?' he asked harshly. 'What do you mean by breakin' in here like this?'

'I know you,' said Hester tightly, without waiting for Bob to speak. 'You're Bob Nevin. You gone plumb loco, ridin' into Aracoa like this?'

'Not a chance,' Bob said flatly. 'I know what I'm doin'.'

'Nevin!' said the judge. His brows drew together in a calculating look. 'You're the killer I signed a warrant for. Wanted in connection with the killing of a man in Benson. Broken out of jail by a bunch of outlaws. So you did ride back to the Circle Four. I had the feelin' you were too smart for that.'

'Then you guessed wrong, didn't you?' Bob grinned

114

faintly, but the barrel of the gun in his hand did not waver by so much as an inch. 'I made up my mind as soon as I heard about this crooked deal that's been goin' on between you and Clayton that I'd have to do somethin' about it.'

Hester gave a harsh bark of a laugh. 'In less than twenty-four hours, you and those other folk will be dead, Nevin. Make no mistake about that. Clayton will send his whole crew against you. You've signed your death warrant by comin' back and tryin' to fight him.'

'Reckon we'll see about that,' Bob said grimly. 'So far, we seem to have held our own and now that most of the ranchers have decided to throw in their lot with us, Clayton is goin' to have a real fight on his hands. He won't be able to go around rustlin' cattle and shootin' down men from ambush this time.'

'You can't get away with takin' the law into your own hands,' Judge Mender said. He smiled faintly. 'Now why don't you see sense, Nevin. You're an intelligent man. I'm quite sure that if I was to have a word with Mister Clayton, he'd overlook this lapse on your part, might even consider allowin' your father to stay on at the Circle Four. The mining company doesn't want to take over all of this territory. There'll be a greater place for those ranchers who help us. Clayton is the sort of man who doesn't forget a good turn.'

'I'm not that big a fool,' Bob said thinly. 'Besides, I don't like the way you operate.' He turned his whole attention to the sheriff. 'Turn round, Hester and face the wall yonder.'

The man hesitated, then turned slowly, his hands still lifted. He was half turned from Bob when the other brought the barrel of his gun against the side of the sheriff's head. Hester crashed to the floor without a sound and lay still.

'You'll pay for this, Nevin. First cold-blooded murder – and now this.'

Bob's answering smile was grim. 'You know damned well that charge of murder against me was trumped-up. Besides,

I figure I know who shot Duffield in the back. But I've got other things on my mind at the moment apart from arguin' with you.'

Mender looked down at the unconscious figure of the sheriff, then back at the gun in Bob's hand and ran the tip of his tongue over dry lips. 'I don't have anythin' to do with killers,' he said hoarsely. His voice was a little more than a dry whisper, like a ball of tumbleweed drifting against the dust of some empty street.

'Seems to me that you're on mighty friendly terms with a whole bunch of them,' Bob said tightly. 'I refer to Clayton and his hired gunslingers. They've already killed three of my father's hands, and burned out the Killearns and last night they got more than they bargained for that time.'

He saw the sudden spark of quick interest at the back of the other's eyes, knew that this was something Mender had not been told. 'What has that got to do with me?' the judge asked faintly. 'I'm here to give court rulings on any cases brought before me. And as I see it, the law is quite plain in this instance. Vergil Clayton brought deeds which had been filed by the mining company on this land here. So far as I've been able to discover, the deeds which the ranchers and homesteaders claim to have are not legal. They never formally filed claim to that land.'

'The land was given to them by the Government after the war and you know that as well as I do, without having to cloak it all in your legal jargon. Only what interests me at the moment is how much you're gettin' from Clayton for holdin' up the course of true justice. He's makin' damned sure that nobody gets through to Dallas to fight this in the County law court, because he knows that he'd lose the case, so he's got to resort to bluff and violence. Otherwise he'd have no call to bring in these hardcases, who only know one law, that of the gun. Your job was to see that the court here threw out any case brought before it on behalf of these people in the territory. I'm figurin' that you're gettin paid for this, Mender, and also that there's an agreement someplace here, safely locked away. Knowing both you and Clayton, you wouldn't trust each other an inch, so it's got to be in writing.'

For a second, the look of fear was clearly visible on the other's features and in spite of the tight grip he tried to get on himself, Bob saw his eyes flick momentarily to the small picture which hung on the wall behind the padded desk.

He smiled grimly, moved forward and prodded the other in the side with the barrel of the gun. 'So that's where you've got it,' he said sharply. 'Reckon that you'd better get it out quick. Otherwise I may decide that Aracoa is better off without a crooked judge like you.'

The other uttered a gasp of agony as the barrel ground into his ribs. There were beads of sweat on his forehead and trickling down his cheeks. He took a hesitant step forward. then stopped.

'Don't you think you're bein' very rash and foolish,' he muttered. 'All you have to do is walk out of here and forget anythin' you know, and you can be a very rich man. You won't stop the company when it really starts. Why not see sense and get on to the winnin' side?'

'Because there are some people I don't think ought to live and Vergil Clayton is one of them,' Bob answered tightly. He pressed a little harder with the gun, urging the other forward. 'Now get that safe open – and fast!'

CHAPTER EIGHT

CROOKED DEAL

Judge Mender paused in front of the picture, then tilted it slightly to one side, revealing the safe set, as Bob had supposed, in the wall. He paused then, half turned his head.

'All right, open it and take out the papers,' Bob ordered.

'I still say that you're a fool,' muttered the other thickly. 'Ten thousand dollars. There could be as much as that in it for you if you'll join us. Once we've taken over the entire valley, ain't no reason why you shouldn't get the spread back, in time, and with that sort of money, you could become the most powerful man in the territory.'

'And what would happen to the others in the meantime?'

The other shrugged. 'Somebody always has to go under,' he said callously. 'It's the way of progress. The weakest go to the wall and only the strong are fit to survive.'

'Open that safe,' Bob grated tautly. 'I won't tell you again.' His finger tightened on the trigger and thinking took a hungry, angry shape on his mouth. He would not have thought twice about shooting this man down, there and then, but he might still need him.

Mender straightened, fumbled in his pocket for a small bunch of keys, selected one of them and leaned forward to fit it into the lock of the safe. He opened it slowly, swinging the heavy steel door aside and over his shoulder. Bob could

118

make out the papers and the wads of dollar bills carefully stacked away inside. He reckoned that there must have been several thousand dollars there.

'So you keep your ill-gotten gains in there too,' he said through tight lips. 'I wonder how much of that really belongs to the ranchers whose cattle was rustled and whose crops were destroyed.'

The other said nothing, but reached in and grasped a pile of the papers in the middle of the safe. Then, without warning, he swung from the waist, throwing the papers in Bob's eyes at the same time, slamming downward with his hand at the other's wrist. The sudden move took Bob completely by surprise. The gun was knocked from his hand and went skidding across the floor to end up in the far corner of the room. At the same moment, Mender whirled. There was an incredible strength in his body as he threw himself forward, clawed fingers reaching for the other's eyes.

Bob fell back in front of the fury of the other's attack until he felt the side of the small desk in his back. A savage blow caught him on the side of the head, pain jarring redly into his skull. Instinctively, he rolled to one side as a second punch came in, managed to take it on his upraised forearm, riding the sting from the blow. His head was ringing from the jarring effect of that first punch and a second later, the other recovering his balance, jumped forward, thrusting his head against Bob's chest, then bringing it up sharply so that the top of his skull cracked with a stunning force under Bob's chin. The blow roared through his brain and dimly, he heard the other's harsh, guttering breathing as he moved back.

Sucking air down into his lungs, Bob forced himself to keep his eyes open and look about him. The other was some distance away from him, had made no attempt to follow up his advantage. Then Bob saw why. Mender had the drawer of the desk open and he was scrabbling inside it for the loaded derringer. At that moment, Bob wished fervently that he had taken the weapon when he had the chance.

He saw the sudden look of triumph on the other's shadowed face as his fingers closed around the weapon and he jerked it out of the drawer. Another moment and Bob knew it would be levelled on him and the other would not hesitate to pull the trigger, shooting to kill. He would have the perfect alibi. Bob had broken into the place with intent to steal valuable documents. The sheriff would back up that statement and then he had made an attempt to kill Mender. Everyone in town would believe that Mender had fired in self-defence and even though he did not, his father and the other ranchers would not be able to prove a thing.

He acted instinctively and in doing so, saved his life. The judge's finger was already tightening on the trigger when he caught his hands under the edge of the desk and jerked it upward with all of the strength in his body. It lifted from the floor, tilted, then crashed back against the other, sending him staggering against the wall.

Before he could recover his balance, Bob was around the overturned desk, snatching at the other's wrist, bending it back until he was forced to drop the Derringer with a yelp of agony. Mender twisted savagely, striving to wriggle from Nevin's grasp. His mouth was open, eyes bulging from his head as rage and fear surged through him.

Bob waited, then grabbed at the other's arm and hauled him out from behind the desk. His fist travelled less than six inches but it caught the other flush on the point of the jaw. Mender's legs collapsed like rubber under him and he slumped back against the upturned desk, his eyes glassy, hanging there with all of the fight knocked out of him.

He recovered a few minutes later, his mouth hanging slackly open, his breath gushing in and out through his teeth. He rubbed his jaw gingerly, wincing as pain went through his head.

'Now you know that I mean what I say,' Bob told him. He

picked up some of the papers scattered on the floor, glancing through them carefully in the yellow lamplight, keeping a watch on the other, although he expected little trouble from him after the beating he had taken. Finally, he came across the paper he had been searching for.

'Just like I figured,' he said softly, folding it and placing it in his pocket. 'Thieves never seem able to trust each other. Guess it's a law of nature.'

'All right,' snarled the other, rubbing his bleeding lips. 'What do you intend to do now? You know that you'll never get back to the Circle Four ranch alive and even if you do, Clayton is goin' to send all of his men against you. You're goin' to regret this night's work, believe me.'

Bob shook his head. 'Somehow I don't think so. I've got enough here to blow your little scheme wide open and you know it. But just in case there are a few of Clayton's men around the town or along the trail back, I intend to take you with me. You'll make an excellent shield.'

He saw the look of fear on the judge's face, knew this was the first time that the possibility of this had occurred to the other. Mender's glance flicked wildly from side to side, like that of a trapped animal seeking some way of escape, but knowing that it would find none.

Moving back from the other, Bob retrieved his gun from the corner of the room, checked it, then nodded to the other. 'All right – outside! I figure your mount is there together with Hester's.'

'What about the sheriff?' queried the other. He was evidently trying to stall for time, hoping that somebody else might come along and butt into Bob's play, and give him a chance to escape.

'He'll stay here until somebody finds him,' Bob said sharply. He motioned with the Colt, indicating the outer door. 'Now move. And any funny move on your part will be your last. I won't have the slightest hesitation about shootin' you down.'

121

Mender sucked in a sharp breath, rubbed his sleeve over his face, smearing the blood over his cheeks. His swollen eyes and the dull purple bruises which were just beginning to show under the mottled flesh gave him a hard, vicious look but he went ahead of Bob, opened the door as the other extinguished the lamp and stepped outside. There were a couple of horses tethered to the small hitching rail on the rough ground.

'Walk your horse with me,' Bob ordered as the other made to swing up into the saddle.

A look of surprise appeared on the other's swollen face, but he did not question the other and taking up the reins, walked slowly with Bob to the mouth of the narrow alley that cut back from the main street. Five minutes later, they were both mounted and riding out the outskirts of Aracoa. There was a moon just rising above the eastern horizon, throwing a pale eerie glow over the roofs of the silent houses, shops and stores. It was a cold light, having no warmth of its own and Bob felt a little shiver run through him as the cold air, descending from the upper slopes of the mountains across the plains, blew against him.

Mender sat hunched forward in the saddle, his face drooping on to his chest, hands gripping the reins tightly. He seemed resigned to what had happened to him but Bob was not fooled by this. He knew that somewhere in that scheming mind, Mender was calculating some way of getting himself out of this mess before Bob could get him to the Circle Four. Once he was there, his chance of getting away was very remote.

The land grew more rugged as they climbed up through the moonlit rocks and they moved out of one canyon into another, higher and higher along the edge of the cliff as the moon rose into the clear heavens, giving them plenty of light by which to see. But the land itself was deceptive. The pathway dropped down the face of the cliff at a breakneck angle, running lower and lower so that they were forced to ride their mounts stiff-legged, bracing themselves in the stirrups, leaning back to enable their horses to maintain their balance. Bob half expected the other to make a break for it along this stretch of trail, when he was more concerned with keeping his balance than watching Mender, but the judge had evidently decided that there was little point in risking his own neck along this treacherous stretch of the trail, where the first false step would mean instant death on the jagged peaks of the rocks down below.

Turning to the other, Bob said: 'I figure there's a better way of movin' down off this ridge, Mender. You know of it?'

'No,' replied the other shortly. His tone implied that even if he did, he did not intend to give the information to Bob.

The long, twisting trail ended finally as they rode out of the trail boulder-strewn foothills on to the smooth flatness of the plain. At the first convenient spot they cut away from the trail where it began to angle back in the direction of the hills and headed out across the prairie. They made a way through a stand of timber and eventually came to a point where they could look across the moonlit scrub to where the low hills that fronted the Circle Four spread lifted in a humped line on the distant horizon.

'There's the Circle Four spread,' Bob said tightly. 'If you've got any ideas about tryin' to make a break for it better forget 'em right now, I'll shoot you before you can cover a dozen yards.'

Noticing the fractional slump of the other's shoulders, he guessed that Mender had been thinking along these lines all the way through the hills. Now it had been brought home to him how little a chance he really had, unless they bumped into a bunch of Clayton's men out here.

Their way was level for five miles or more with the country gradually growing less rough; and afterwards the trail made a swift sweep to the north-west, parallelling the low hills for a little way before swinging back towards them. Another two hours brought them up into the lower slopes, and then through the thicker timber, the carpet of pine needles muffling the sound of their horses. Beyond the timber, the trail grew broader and better; and presently it fell into the road that led down through the rocks to the Circle Four. They were halfway along it and Bob was watching the rocky upthrusts closely on either side, still feeling that sense of unease that had been with him most of the night. He saw nothing. Yet quite suddenly, there was the ominous click of a rifle bolt and a man's voice called softly:

'Identify yourselves. Don't make a reach for your guns.'

Bob, startled, then smiled faintly. It was the man on guard, the man he had passed on his way out of the ranch.

'It's me, Bob Nevin,' he called back. 'I've got me a prisoner. Judge Mender from Arocoa.'

A pause, then the other called out. 'Bring him up, Bob, so I can have a look at him.'

Evidently the other was taking no chances, Bob thought. The realization gave him a feeling of relief. At last, the chances of anybody getting through to the ranch were pretty small.

'Has there been any trouble durin' the night?' Bob asked the man as they rode up.

The other shook his head in the moonlight. 'Everythin' been quiet,' he averred. 'A couple more families rode in a little before midnight. Seems the word has got around what you're tryin' to do. We expect more might ride in before mornin'.'

'Well, at least now we know where we stand,' Bob replied. 'Clayton isn't goin' to wait any longer than he can help once he hears of this. He'll know that the longer he delays before making his move, the stronger we'll become, and that is one thing he can't afford to allow.'

'Like I told you, Nevin,' sneered Mender. 'You don't have a chance. Do you think these hicks that have ridden in

124

tonight will stand up against seasoned gunmen?'

'So you're admittin' now that Clayton has brought in gunhawks just for the purpose of drivin' these folk off the range.'

'All right, so it's true,' snarled the judge. 'But you'll soon discover that you can't do anythin' about it.'

'If I were you, I'd remember that whether Clayton over-rides us or not, there's a bullet waitin' for you.' His tone was perfectly serious as he spoke and Mender's face blanched. 'Now ride ahead of me to the ranch-house.'

There was a grave expression on Ben Nevin's face as Bob rode in, dismounted, then forced Mender to walk ahead of him into the house. He said quietly: 'We've got close on a score of men ready to ride with us, Bob. What's your plan of action?'

'Whatever we do, we've got to move fast. I'd hoped that we might be able to hold off a couple of days at least, to build up our strength and see how the land lies, but although the town was quiet tonight, with bringin' Mender here and havin' to knock the sheriff out, I figure that Clayton will know what has happened before dawn and he'll come ridin' at once.'

'We'll be outnumbered. I suppose you already know that, and whether the mettle of the men we have will be enough, is anybody's guess,' said the older man cautiously.

'That bein' the case, I reckon the only hope we have is to carry out a series of attacks on them before they get here. This is as good a defensive spot as any there is, but we wouldn't be able to hold out for very long before we ran short of food and ammunition.'

'You think that the sheriff will bring a posse and throw them in behind Clayton and his band?' The other drew his bushy brows into a straight line.

'Maybe. There ain't no doubt that his pride will have been hurt by what happened tonight and a man like that will take any affront as a call to action. But I'm not so sure he'll get much support from the town. They've never liked this attack by the mining company on the outlyin' ranches. This was a peaceful place before they arrived and the shop-keepers must be losin' a lot of profit, even though the mining boys buy some supplies from them.'

'So we can count on facin' Clayton's bunch and possibly one or two hotheads who may decide to follow the sheriff,' murmured Ben Nevin soberly.

'That's about it,' Bob agreed.

'When were you figurin' on ridin' out with some of the men? You'll be leavin' some behind to watch the ranch.'

'As soon as they can saddle up, we'll pull out. First I'll get a bite to eat. No tellin' when we'll get another meal. If we can hit 'em as they cut through the hills, we may be able to finish a few of them and lead the others away into the desert.'

He turned, went into the house. June Dawney was up, busying herself in the kitchen.

'Don't take any risks, Bob,' she said when he told her what his plans were. She laid a hand on his arm. 'Everyone in the valley is depending on you now. And I want you to come back for myself.'

Bob nodded, felt a little thrill run through him. 'I'll remember that, June,' he said softly. 'You'll be runnin' a risk too, simply by stayin' here. Clayton may guess what we mean to do and he'll play clever, splitting his force and sending one on here while the other keeps a watch along the main trail.'

He seated himself at the table and a few moments later, a plate of stew was put down to him, with several slices of corn bread and a cup of hot coffee. He ate ravenously, the food acting as a stimulant, making him feel more alive, anxious to meet up with Clayton, strike a blow against the other.

By the time he had finished, the men who were riding with him had mounted up and were waiting in the courtyard. Some were smoking, others talking among themselves in low voices. He could feel the tension in the air as he walked down from the porch, made his way over to them, his spurs dragging up the dust of the courtyard. Tightening his lips into a hard, firm line, he swung up into the saddle, raised his hand to June Dawney where she stood in the doorway, a slim figure outlined against the yellow lamp glow. Then he kicked spurs to his mount and they thundered out of the courtyard, up towards the trail that led through the low hills.

As they rode over the crest and down the other side, past the small herd with two cowboys riding around the perimeter of the sleeping animals, Bob glanced at the men who rode with him, their faces in half shadow, their mouths and eyes grim with determination. How many of these men would ride back with him if they succeeded in hitting Clayton's men without warning? he wondered tensely. Would he be coming back himself? He did not doubt that some would be killed. In a range war such as this, it was inevitable that there should be casualties. Whenever there was something worth having, it seemed that men had to die for it, that sacrifices had to be made for it. Nothing worthwhile was obtained easily.

Dawn found them riding through the heavy timber on the middle slopes of the tall hills. The grey light was just beginning to filter through the trees as they splashed over a narrow stream, then paused to give their horses a chance to blow. They had encountered no one on the trail during the three hours they had been riding and over everything there had hung a deep and suppressed quiet that gradually began to grate on the nerves, stretching them taut through the body, rubbing them raw. The slightest untoward movement brought men's heads wringing sharply around, sent hands diving for gunbutts. More often than not, it was merely the faint movement of some nocturnal animal in the thickly tangled brush under the trees, disturbed by their presence.

Before they moved out again, Bob cautioned the men to silence, then gigged his mount forward and lifted his hand to explain what their objective was and how they were to go about achieving it.

'There's a long, low ridge about a mile from here,' he explained, 'that stands out some two hundred feet above the trail. If we can get up there and watch for them comin' we may be able to start a landslide that will be enough to throw them into confusion while the rest of us pick them off with the rifles. But remember, everybody. Once we're up there, I don't want a shot fired, intentionally or otherwise. until those rocks have started fallin'. Now let's mount up and take a look over the place.'

In the grey light of dawn, the rocks looked bare and gaunt where they towered over the trail. Sitting tall in the saddle, Bob surveyed them intently, running his glance along the sharply-pointed spires of rock that clawed at the grey dawn sky. There was a narrow trail which led up to one end of the ledge he had spotted earlier. They would have to lead their horses up there, but there was nowhere else they could leave them without running the risk of having them seen by Clayton's men before they reached the spot immediately below where he intended to start the landslide.

He switched his glance to the other side of the trail. Here the ground was more open but still broken up by rugged boulder formations which would, he reckoned, provide an excellent place where a small group of men could hide and still be out of the way of the crashing landslide when it hit the trail, burying it under tons of boulders and powdered stone.

He called Matt over to him. 'Matt, I want you to take five men and station yourselves in the rocks yonder, about fifty feet away from the edge of the trail where you'll be away from the flying rocks once we start 'em movin'. I figure that you ought to be able to cover the trail for nearly a quarter of a mile in either direction and that should give you the chance to pick off any who try to go under cover once we start firin' from up there.' He pointed to the ledge above

128

the trail. We're not goin' to give them a chance, so shoot to kill. But wait for the slide to start before you open up. We don't want to give 'em any advance warnin'.'

The other nodded. 'I understand.' He motioned to his group to follow him and led the way into the rocks. Bob called the others together, directed them to dismount and lead their horses along the twisting, narrow trail that led up the steep side of the rock. Fifteen minutes later, they reached the ledge which was some ten feet wide and wound around the rock for more than four hundred feet before petering out. It was hemmed in by the boulders on both sides, affording them plenty of cover so that it would be virtually impossible for them to be seen from below. The boulders that edged the ledge looked as though they could be prised loose with some little effort.

Spreading the men out along the ledge, with the horses tethered together at one point, they crouched down, settling themselves to wait. Leaning his back against the rocky wall behind him, Bob rolled a cigarette, thrust it between his lips, and lit it with a sulphur match, drawing the sweet-tasting smoke down into his lungs. As yet, there was no way of telling how long they would have to wait before Clayton and his men came along this particular stretch of the trail. There was, of course, always the possibility that they would not use this trail to the Circle Four, but it was by far the shortest and the best and he guessed that Clayton would be in a hurry to strike his blow and get his punch in first. That was what Bob was gambling on.

The man beside Bob lifted his head cautiously and peered along the trail in the brightening daylight. He shrugged his shoulders as he sank back on to his haunches again. 'No sign of anybody there,' he grunted. 'You sure they'll come this way?'

'Hell, I'm not sure of anythin' that Clayton might do,' Bob said tensely. He forced evenness into his voice, realized that he was allowing the tension to get the better of him. 'But it seems reasonable that if he wants to get his men to the Circle Four quickly, this is the way he has to come. Any other trail would take him in a wide detour that would add miles and hours to the journey and I'm sure that in his present frame of mind, he'll be in a goddamned hurry.'

'I hope you're right,' murmured the other, taking out his Colt and checking the barrel and cylinders. 'It's goin' to be hotter than the hinges of hell once that sun gets up and this ain't likely to be the coolest spot on the trail.'

Bob glanced across the wide valley. The sun had just lifted clear of the horizon, a vast red ball that glared with fiery light but no heat as yet. There were no clouds visible in the sky and it promised to be another scorching, blistering day.

An hour passed. Still the tight, pendant silence clung to the scene. The trail, where it wound down the lee of the hills, remained empty. There was no dust cloud to indicate the presence of a group of hard riding men, pushing their mounts to the utmost. Had Clayton proved to be too clever for him? Had he ridden around the hills, knowing that a watch might be kept on this trail and that if he was to take the defenders of the Circle Four ranch by surprise, he would have to swing around and take them from a totally unexpected direction? For a moment, indecision was strong within him. If that were so, then the men defending the ranch-house would be overwhelmed. Everything depended on cutting down the number of men that Clayton had to back his play and this seemed to be the only way they had of doing it. But if their luck was dead against them. . . .

The heat had began to grow in its piled up intensity as the hours passed. The glaring heat struck at the rocks around them with a burning touch, the harsh glare reflected into their eyes no matter how they tried to shield them from it. Looking at the sun, Bob judged that it would soon be noon. If the bunch from Aracoa had not appeared by then, he would be forced to assume they had already attacked the ranch from a direction which he had not expected.

130

CHAPTER NINE

LANDSLIDE!

It was now almost the height of the day and the noon heat lay over the land like the pressure of a mighty fist, fierce and unrelenting. The sun blazed down from the cloudless blue mirror of the sky, washing all of the colour from the rocks and the few stunted trees which managed to survive there in the arid, thin soil. Wiping the sweat from his brow, Bob squinted into the shimmering heat haze and tried to watch the spot where the narrow trail wound around a bend some five hundred yards away. The rest of the men lay enduring the merciless heat, occasionally throwing a quick, speculative glance in his direction, probably wondering whether he knew what he was doing, whether he may have miscalculated what Clayton would do.

Bob too, was beginning to have doubts. Surely, he argued with himself, Clayton would have been warned of what had happened by now. Hester would have recovered consciousness and would have lost no time in telling the other that Bob had been in town, that he must have taken Mender prisoner to the Circle Four and also that the ranchers were rallying around the Nevins, determined to fight it out to the finish. So why was Clayton delaying so long? Was he unsure of the strength of the opposition, not wanting to lose more of his men in an attempt to smash the Circle Four?

The man next to him pulled the brim of his hat further down over his eyes in an attempt to shut out the glaring, dizzying sunlight, lifted his head a little to reach for his water bottle, then paused with it halfway to his lips.

'There they are,' he said hoarsely. He dropped the canteen and pointed.

Cautiously, Bob peered through a narrow cleft in the rocks. At first, the harsh sunlight dazzled him so much that he could see nothing and the throbbing pain at the back of his eyes made it even more difficult. Then, gradually, he picked out the bunch of men spurring their mounts along the trail, the dust cloud kicked up by their horses' hoofs hanging in the still air behind them.

'That's them all right,' he agreed. 'Get ready behind these rocks. When I give the signal send 'em rollin'.'

'You reckon that'll be enough?'

Bob nodded. 'Most of the stuff below this ledge is loose shale. It'll all go once the boulders start down.'

The men drifted apart and crouched down out of sight behind the tall boulders, waiting to do their deadly work. Through the rocks in front of him he watched the line of advancing men anxiously. There were close on a score of them, he estimated, riding fast considering the treacherous surface of the trail. He tried to make out the figure of Vergil Clayton, but could see no sign of him. It was just possible that he would want to be in at the kill. Grimly, Bob hoped that he would have the chance to get the other in the sights of his rifle.

The riders came on without faltering, evidently expecting no trouble. This was ideal country for an ambush, yet they did not seem to have considered the possibility. Bob grinned to himself. Then they were soon going to discover how fatal a mistake this could be. He hoped that none of the men on the far side of the trail would get an itchy trigger finger and fire off a shot before he was ready. A lot was going to depend on split second timing here. The landslide had to be started at just the right moment and nothing must warn those men down there that they were riding to their doom.

They came on at a swift pace, the dust following them. Now they were so close that he could make out some of their faces in the bright sunlight, but he saw nothing of Vergil Clayton.

Apart from the thunder of hoofs on the hard rock as the riders approached, the silence was an oppressive thing and the tense seconds fleeted by while the men watched with bated breath, their hands resting on the rough stone, their backs and legs braced, ready to thrust forward as soon as Bob gave the word. He eyed them closely for a moment, noticing the expressions of grim determination on their faces. These were men he could trust right to the very end, he thought thankfully.

Less than a hundred yards away, the trail straightened out, ran like an arrow through the towering rocks on either side. He waited until the last man had entered that particular stretch, threw a swift glance to either side of him, then yelled harshly, giving the order. The men thrust with all their strength. One by one, the boulders were prised loose from the stone, teetering on the lip of the steep slope for a second before sliding down. Rocks, disturbed after countless centuries, bounded downward, carrying down the smaller stones and boulders in their path. The roar of the landslide increased until it was a booming thunder in their ears, the ground trembling beneath their feet.

Smaller rocks were pulled from the slope and an entire section of the rock face was set in motion as the landslide started, its tremendous momentum carrying it down at an ever-increasing pace. The mighty roar swelled until it blotted out everything. Through the cloud of dust that lifted immediately beneath their position, Bob was able to see several of the riders lift their heads, their faces pale grey blurs as they stared up at the terrible destruction which was sweeping down upon them, immense and irresistible. There was no way of escape for most of the men. The landslide engulfed them completely, sweeping them across the trail, crushing them against the solid wall of rock on the other side.

The few who did manage to race out of the way of it were caught by the gunfire that splashed from the rocks where Matt and his men were waiting. Just as the first rocks crashed down on that section of the trail, Bob saw the first five men in the column spur their mounts forward madly to escape from the death which hurtled down on them from above. The men swung clear, diving from their saddles into the cover of the rocks as the landslide came down like a vast moving carpet, blotting out men and horses. Ton upon ton of rock and dust lay piled on top of each other.

Then the slide was over, having ground itself to a halt and the dust began to settle slowly. There was still need for caution as Bob signalled the men to move downward. Some of the men had undoubtedly escaped destruction and had gone to cover among the rocks. But the tense silence which settled over the men as they began to edge their way forward came mostly from the awesome shock they had experienced on seeing that terrible wall of rock pulverize the trail and everything which had been on it at the moment when it had struck.

Going down the slope on his heels, feeling the loose earth slide beneath him, Bob reached the trail a few yards from where it had been engulfed by the rocks, stared about him for a moment, listening to the shots which came from the other side, then ran for the rocks ahead of him. A slug spanged off the rock within inches of his head and a moment later, a ragged volley crashed out from further along the trail and bullets followed him as he dived urgently for cover.

He crawled along the rocks for a little way, moving slowly so as not to attract the attention of the gunman, worming his way around the boulders, moving from shadow to shadow.

Ahead of him, there was a narrow wrinkle in the ground and without hesitation, he lowered himself into it, his gun in his right hand. His legs jarred as he hit the bottom, almost losing his balance. Then, almost before he was aware of his danger, he turned to find a man standing less than five feet away. The other had already turned at the sound of Bob's approach and his gun was lining up on the other's chest, finger tightening on the trigger. There was a vicious grin on his face. Bob knew that he could not hope to beat the other to the draw now. Instead, he acted instinctively, lowering his head and propelling himself forward with a savage thrust of his legs. His lowered head hit the other in the stomach, just below the breastbone, knocking all of the air from his lungs in a sharp whoosh, driving him back against the rock behind him. The killer still kept his hold on the gun in his hand, but before he could free himself from Bob's entangling embrace and bring it up to use it, Bob had slashed savagely with his own revolver at the other's wrist. With a shriek of pain the man dropped the gun, clutched at his wrist, and swung. His elbow caught Bob on the arm, deflecting his aim and the bullet whined off the solid rock, went ricocheting into the distance with the thin, high-pitched wail of tortured metal.

Clenching his left fist, Bob hammered a couple of swift, stabbing blows at the other, sending him staggering back. But the man twisted his arms around Bob's middle, pinning his arms to his sides, making it impossible for him to use his gun. They crashed to the rocky floor of the small dust bowl and rolled together in a threshing tangle of limbs.

Savagely, Bob tried to break the other's hold, but the man held on with a desperate, superhuman strength, knowing that he was fighting for his life. With an urgency born of desperation, he tried to bring up his knee into Bob's groin, but the other saw the move coming and twisted himself swiftly to one side so that the blow grazed along his thigh, doing little damage. The man was a dirty fighter as Bob had expected. Lunging up with his right knee, he managed to throw the man off, although the gunman still held his arms pinned to his sides. Kicking with his heel, he caught the other on the ankle, heard the man grunt with pain and loosen his hold a little. It was all that Bob needed. Jerking his arms aside, he freed them, swung inward with his fingers straightened, the double blow catching the man on both sides of the neck. His eyes stared from his head and he uttered a low bleat of pain as his head fell back, striking the rock behind him with a sickening thud.

Gasping air down into his heaving lungs, Bob got to his feet, stood swaying for a moment as he fought to clear his throbbing head. The man lay limp on the hot rock and bending, Bob lifted his arm, then shook the other's shoulder, felt the unmistakable looseness about him, knew that he was dead. The blow had broken his neck as if it had been a matchstick.

Moving over the lifeless body of the gunhawk, Bob picked up his fallen Colt, checked it, then stepped to the rocks, glancing about him. The roll of gunfire seemed to echo on all sides of him now and it was soon evident that, although from up on the ledge it had appeared that most of the riders had been trapped and buried in that slide of rock and dirt, quite a number of them were still alive, crouched down among the rocks, and their fire was becoming more deadly and accurate as the minutes went on and the first shock of stunned surprise faded. He reckoned that they were probably about evenly matched now. The only advantage he and his men had was that they were sited on both sides of the trail and could take the scattered gunmen from two directions.

Searching with eyes and ears, he tried to determine the direction from which the heaviest concentration of gunfire came. Most of it seemed to be originating from the cluster of tumbled rocks less than a dozen yards from him and he leaned forward to peer through the rocks, searching out the hidden gunmen. There was a tight feeling in his chest as he leaned against the sun-scorched rock, his pulse was racing and his heart pounded painfully against his ribs. There was a faint fluttering sensation in the pit of his stomach and as he tightened his grip on the Colt, he felt it slippery with sweat where his palm rested against the smooth wood of the butt.

Drawing in a deep breath in an attempt to ease the pumping thump of his heart, he glanced round swiftly to see the three men who moved out from the cover of the rocks, cutting slantwise across his field of vision. They were all Clayton's men, so intent on shifting their position that they had not spotted him there. Bob triggered a quick shot at them, saw one man go down. The return fire from the other two was immediate, smashing back even as Bob hurled himself sideways. Two muzzles followed Bob's rapid movement, belching smoke and flame. Bob fired even as he threw himself flat. Splinters of rock stung his face as he came up on one knee, searching through the blue haze of gunswoke for any sign of the two men. He felt the hot breath of a passing slug, ducked instinctively, then lifted himself and fired all in the same movement. He saw one of the rannies jerk, try to prop himself up against one of the rocks, resting all of his sagging weight on one arm, the other struggling to lift the gun which seemed to be too heavy for him. He almost made it. Then the strength seemed to drain from his body with the blood that oozed down the front of his skirt. He fell forward on to his face and the third man, eyes wide as he saw his two companions cut down, darted behind one of the rocks, twisting suddenly, as he strove to get out of reach of the slugs that would come reaching for him at any second.

The seconds ticked by. Bob listened intently for any sound of movement among the rocks where the gunman had gone do earth. for a long moment there was nothing. Then his ears caught the sound of a harsh intake of breath as the other, unable to contain himself, gave away his position by his need to breathe. Bob grinned to himself in the hot sunlight, dashed the sweat from his forehead with the back of his left hand, and moved around the rocks, circling behind the hidden gunslinger. A glinting rifle barrel puffed smoke and flame from a position further away on the far side of the trail and a snarling bullet broke stone from a rock close to Bob's head as he glided forward.

By the time he came out into the open behind the third gunman, the other had shifted his position again. Evidently, he had taken the stillness to mean that Bob was trying to trap him and although he could not see the other, he had decided against remaining where he was. Lifting his head slowly, Bob peered down into the sea of boulders that stretched away in front of him. He could just make out the legs of one of the men he had killed, but there was no sign of the third man.

Dimly, Bob could hear Matt's loud voice yelling orders in the distance, rallying some of the men who were wilting in the face of the heavy, accurate lead thrown by the gunhawks. If they broke and ran now, it would mean the end. Desperately, Bob searched around for the rest of his men, saw a small bunch of them crouched in a narrow opening among the rocks, firing desultorily at the gunmen. Close by, he caught sight of the tall figure of Matt, waving his arms, urging them forward.

He moved silently forward, eyes alert. There were no

tangible enemies now. Only the darting flashes of gunfire from the rocks and the crashing reverberations that echoed from the overhanging ledges, magnifying the sound a hundredfold. The sound and the flashes were confusing to the ear and eye; and slugs whined through the harsh, glaring sunlight, hitting rock and yielding flesh alike, bringing death here and there where men cursed and died on their feet, while others, more fortunate merely felt the hot bite of it in their bodies, knew they had been hit and lay where they fell.

The gunmen had rallied now. There were two groups of them, separated by perhaps thirty yards, on either side of the place where the avalanche of rock had smashed down on the trail, blotting it out of existence. Nearly half a dozen guns pumped lead at Bob's fleeting figure as he ran through the rocks to where the men were crouched down with Matt.

There he was abreast of the other, clambered over a couple of tall, upthrusting boulders and dropped down on to the smoother ground beyond as two slugs whined through the air where his head had been a split second before. The gunfire continued in a chaotic racket of sound, hurting on the eardrums. Hoarse voices were shouting all around Bob as he crawled forward to join the men, pinned down by the gunfire.

'All right,' he yelled. 'We've finished more than half of them. Now we'll either kill the rest or drive them off. Shoot to kill.'

His words rallied them, heightened their spirits. Several of the gunmen, believing that it was all over and they had crushed the last spark of resistance, got to their feet, showed themselves in blurred silhouette as they ran forward over the rocks. Aiming rapidly, Bob pumped shot after shot into the attackers, watched as they fell, then pulled back on the retreat.

Bob breathed easier as he crouched down and filled the

empty chambers of his guns with shells from the loops in his belt. The situation was still tense. The men were still penned in, but the enemy had left three of their number sprawled over the rocks after that last attempt.

'They'll come again,' he warned as the men crouched down. 'But I figure that if we can throw them back this time, we've got 'em licked. They'll pull out and head for the Circle Four.'

'But that ain't what we want to happen,' said one of the men sharply. His brow creased in sudden thought – 'or is it?'

'That's right. We let them ride in on the ranch. Once we've got 'em pressed in against the others there, we take them from the rear. Whatever happens, we've got to get them all bunched together and smash this band, once and for all. This is just the preliminary fight, to reduce their numbers so that we fight them on more even terms at the Circle Four.'

'Here they come again,' called one of the other men hoarsely. Bob lifted his head, ducked as a slug richochetted along the V between two of the boulders. There was a sudden outburst of shooting from dead ahead. The gunmen were attempting to rush their position. They came forward, running and crouching, firing from the hip as they came, going down under cover only to reload. Matching shot for shot with the oncoming gunmen, the men in the hollow fired back. The attackers faltered, then they were turning and running. This time, they kept on running to where their horses were waiting along the trail. Bob stood up, loosed off a handful of shots after them as they swung up into the saddle and rode off in a cloud of dust.

Then the shooting stopped. The other group of Clayton's men, trapped by the fall of rock, had found their horses and were moving back along the way they had come.

'I figure that about half a dozen got away towards the

ranch,' Matt said, wiping his sleeve over his face. There was a thin smear of blood on one cheek where a bullet had grazed the skin. He blinked his eyes several times against the harsh sunglare.

'Aren't we goin' after them?' asked one of the other men, thrusting his guns back into leather. 'If we get mounted up we might catch 'em before they get anywhere near the Circle Four spread.'

'We might,' Bob affirmed. 'But that's not what's worryin' me. We've got the wounded to look after and there's no real hurry in goin' after those men. They won't get to the spread much before nightfall and we've done a good job cutting their numbers by as much as we did. 1 figure this is the turning point as far as Clayton's hopes of takin' over control of the territory are concerned.'

'You're right,' Matt nodded. 'That brand of coyote doesn't run far. They'll stop to lick their wounds someplace along the trail, then ride on to join the others. It ain't no part of their orders to try to waylay us along the trail. They know they might get cut to pieces if they did that. We've had a mighty tough battle here and there were times when I figured we weren't goin' to make it in spite of the head start you gave us, Bob, bringin' all that rock down on the trail.'

'It's been rough,' Bob said, rubbing his chin. 'Let's take a look at who's been killed or hurt.'

They made their way among the dead and wounded. Seven of the attackers had been killed in the open. How many lay buried under that rock, it was impossible to estimate. Six perhaps, maybe seven. He did not think many more had been caught by the fall of rock.

Five of their number had been hit, two badly, and three were dead, Bob brought out what first aid kit he carried and Matt tended to the wounded men, patching them up as best he could. He was anxious to get on the move again, but there was no sign of impatience in the way in which he tied

141

up the wounds and made the men as comfortable as he could.

'What do we do with those who're too badly hit to ride with us, Bob?' he asked finally, getting to his feet.

'We leave a couple of the less badly wounded with them,' Bob said without hesitation. 'It's the only choice we have right now. We can't afford to wait any longer.'

'Have you any idea how many men Clayton may have left?'

Bob shrugged. 'I figure he had about fifty on his payroll, but whether they were all gunmen or not, I don't know. Six have got away from this party, and I figure there are probably another twenty-five unaccounted for. They could have headed for the ranch by a different route. He won't have sent all of his men in the one bunch just is case they were ambushed, that means we probably have thirty men against us.'

'That's a lot of men,' said the other soberly.

'This is undoubtedly the showdown. One way or the other, this is going to decide whether good or evil triumphs in this part of the territory.'

Matt's eyes were still troubled as he followed the other up through the rocks to the trail. There was the smell of dust in their nostrils where it still hung in the air and Bob felt it grating against his eyeballs as he climbed into the saddle, waited for the others to mount up, then signalled them to move out.

Vergil Clayton had been in the saddle almost the whole of the day and the dust and heat had only served to increase his irritation. Now he sat stiffly with his legs thrust straight in the stirrups, staring off into the sun-hazed distance. They had ridden a circuitous route since leaving Aracoa, keeping well away from the main stage trail which would be followed by Clinton and the other half of his force. He did not expect to join forces with them until shortly before nightfall at a place less than two miles from the Circle Four ranch-house. Then they would ride in together and finish these people who had decided to make a stand against him.

'There's a stream half a mile away in that direction,' said one of the men. 'I reckon we could rest up there for a while. We've made pretty good time so far.'

'I'll give the orders around here, Forbes,' snapped Clayton angrily. He turned in the saddle, stared at the other for a moment through slitted eyes. Then he gave a brief nod. 'Let's go.'

They moved at a steady canter towards the narrow stand of timber that grew along the bank of the stream which, at this point, came tumbling down the side of the hills from the point where it had been borne, just a little distance above them. Their tired horses, scenting water, increased their pace. Inwardly, Clayton was glad of the opportunity to stop and rest up. The long ride had been gruelling. He was not used to being in the saddle for such a lengih of time, through the full blistering heat of the day, and riding across country as rough as this. But he had been determined to be in at the kill. He now blamed Bob Nevin for all of his misfortunes of the past few days. Ever since the other had showed up at the ranch, things had failed to go right for him. First his men had been beaten off when they had attacked the Dawney place and he had lost several there. Then Nevin had the gall to ride into Aracoa and snatch Mender and possibly some incriminating evidence the other might have, and ride on out of town without any trouble. He gritted his teeth together as he thought of that. What the hell had Hester been doing to allow Nevin to get away with anything like that? The sheriff had admitted that he and the judge had known something was amiss, that a light had been seen in the judge's office. But they had blundered inside without any attempt at caution and been caught on the wrong foot.

Hester would pay for this when he got back to Aracoa, he thought savagely to himself. He could not afford to have inept lawmen in town. Hester had been useful only insomuch that he had been willing to turn a blind eye to anything that had been going on there, so much as he, Clayton, made it worth his while. The time was coming however, when he would need to get a better man for the job.

Sitting by the side of the swift-running stream, he soaked his kerchief in the water and rubbed it over the back of his neck, soothing away some of the heat on his flesh.

As he sat there, he turned over his plans in his mind. With the men he had at his disposal, he felt certain that he could crush any resistance there might be when he arrived at the Circle Four ranch. He did not doubt that throughout the day, other ranchers might have been arriving there, with their hired hands, ready for the coming showdown. His lips drew back over his teeth in a snarl of savage anticipation. He had come a long way over the past few years and he did not intend anyone to stop him from going still further. Born in a small township of less than a dozen houses in Northern Montana, he had been forced to fend for himself during the early years of his life. He had learned the ruthlessness that was to stamp his character in the years to come during those days. Then he had found out for himself that only the strong survived and that the weak and soft went under. He had learned how to handle a gun when he had been only ten years old and although too young when the war had come, he had forseen that there would be action and opportunities out to the west where the country was just being opened up.

He had tried his hand at ranching, but had failed miserably after the first two bad winters, had cut his losses and got out, moving back east. Here, he had met up with the mining company and his ruthlessness had been recognized at an early stage in his career with them. His choice as the man to lead this move to take over this stretch of territory had been almost inevitable. But he knew that he would not stop here. Already, he was looking forward to higher things. But first, he had to finish what he had come here for. These ranchers, headed by the Nevins, had plagued him for too long.

Jerking his mind back to the present, he allowed his gaze to wander over the small clearing. Lighting a cigar, he drew the smoke deeply into his lungs. By now, Nevin would have built up the defences of the ranch as much as possible in the time he'd had at his disposal and Clayton was not such a fool as to think he would have an easy task dislodging them from their defensive position, but he did not doubt for one moment that he would succeed in the end. He could afford to sit it out around the ranch, allowing no one in or out. By the time he was finished, those who were still alive would have to surrender and then he would make an example of them, string them up from the nearest tree. If anyone in Aracoa tried to protest, it would be just too bad. The sooner they learned who was boss around here, the better it would be for all concerned.

CHAPTER TEN

GUNSMOKE SHOWDOWN

Clayton and his men pulled out of the clearing when it lacked one hour from sundown. Already, the sky to the west was aflame with red and twenty minutes later they reached the spot where they had agreed to meet the other group riding along the main stage trail through the hills. As yet, there was no sign of them and Clayton experienced a sense of growing impatience as he sat his mount, peering into the growing dimness, eyes searching for the first sign of them. The ground was reasonably flat here and it seemed almost impossible that they could have been delayed so long. After all, he reckoned, they had had the shortest route to follow even though for part of the way it led through the mountains.

Cal Romaine rode up beside him, shaded his eyes against the red glare, then shook his head in perplexity. 'No sign of them anyway, Mister Clayton,' he said.

Angrily, Clayton snapped: 'I have already noticed that for myself. Somethin' must have happened to delay them. They wouldn't have been this late otherwise.'

'A landslide along the mountain trail perhaps,' suggested the other.

Clayton forced a quick nod. That was what he hoped was the reason, but already, there were other possibilities beginning to form in his mind, ideas that he did not want to think about but which, as the minutes began to tick by, he was forced to take into consideration. Had Nevin been too smart for him and placed an ambushing party somewhere along the trail, ready to jump his men as they rode through? He tried to tell himself that these were men used to the ways of violence and they surely would not be caught unawares like that. Yet something must have happened to prevent them from reaching the rendezvous on time.

He worried and fretted inwardly as he sat there, near the edge of the trail where it forked away across the flat ground. When at length, he spotted the small cloud of dust in the distance, it did little to relieve the sense of growing apprehension in his mind. He tried to tell himself that there was nothing for him to worry about, but inwardly he did not really believe this.

'Doesn't look like a big party,' observed Romaine tightly. 'About half a dozen riders, I'd say from the dust they're raisin'.'

'Then it may not be the boys,' Clayton observed. 'This could be Nevin and some of his men. Get the boys into the trees yonder and be ready to open up as soon as I give the word.'

'Sure.' The other gave the necessary orders and within a minute, all of the men were out of sight among the trees and more than a score of guns were trained on the approaching group of horsemen. The riders reined up as they saw Clayton who had stepped out into the open the moment he recognized them.

'Where are the other men?' he demanded harshly. 'There were close on a score of you when you set out.'

The tall, black-bearded man seated on the chestnut roan said dully, 'We bumped into Nevin and some of his men back there a piece, in the mountains. They started a slide that killed six or seven men outright, then they began firing at us from both sides of the trail, those that were lucky enough not to be caught in the avalanche.'

'And you allowed him to pick you off like sittin' ducks, was that it?' Clayton raged. The veins on his neck stood out under the skin as he swung on the other sharply. He could no longer control the deep-seated anger within that threatened to overwhelm him completely. 'I suppose it never occurred to you that he might try somethin' like that. You just rode blindly into a trap that any child could have forseen.'

'There was no warnin',' muttered the other defensively. 'We took as many of them with us.'

'And where are they now? Ridin' on your heels, I suppose?' There was a deep beat of sarcasm in the other's tone, temporarily drowning out the anger.

'We saw nothin' of them along the trail,' said the other sullenly. 'I figure he can only have half a dozen men with him. The rest are either dead or wounded back there in the hills.'

'And in the meantime, I'm supposed to fight those at the Circle Four with only twenty-five men?'

The other said nothing. He knew that in Clayton's present frame of mind the other could just as easily draw his gun and shoot him down there and then. At length, Clayton forced himself to relax. Things might not be so bad after all. The fact that Nevin had hit his men out in the hills to the south meant that their force had been split too. If he hurried, rode hell for leather to the Circle Four and hit them at dusk, he might still have a good chance of overwhelming the defenders before any help from Nevin's small group could arrive. Turning in the saddle, he began to snap orders to the men. When they finally rode out, they rode at a swift canter, cutting across the grassy plain that bordered the Circle Four spread. Ten minutes later, they came to the perimeter wire, smashed a way through it, trampling it down, and rode into the lush green pastures.

There was no opposition here. Clayton had half expected some but when it became evident there was none, he knew that Ben Nevin had withdrawn all of his men to the ranch, determined to make his stand there.

There was still a little light from the residual glow in the western sky when they rode down out of the stand of trees on top of the low hill and moved cautiously into the open. In the dim light it was possible for them to see that Ben Nevin had prepared the ground well for the coming battle. All of the cover in the courtyard and the ground around the house and barn had been cleared completely. Any boulders which may have been there earlier had been removed, leaving no cover for anyone within two hundred yards of the buildings. This was almost at the limit for a Winchester and Colts were of little use at that range, being highly inaccurate.

Motioning his men into position, he gave the order for them to open fire, aiming for the windows. For the time being, they would have to be content with shooting from the perimeter of this barren zone, at least until they had had a chance of determining the strength of the opposition they were up against.

Glass tinkled from one of the windows and a few moments later, the orange spurts of the return fire were clearly visible on all sides of the house. The final battle for the control of this territory had just begun. . . .

Inside the ranch-house, the defenders had taken up their positions at the windows, so that they could cover every direction of approach. Ben Nevin stood close to the window that looked down into the courtyard, narrowing his eyes to accustom them to the dimness outside. He had already caught sight of a few fleeting shapes close to the skyline beyond the corral, but all of them were still the best part of two hundred yards away and there was little sense in wasting precious ammunition until the attackers came closer, within killing range of their guns.

Across the window from him, Sam Dawney stood with his Springfield cradled in his hands, occasionally moving his head to peer through the glass. His lips were pressed together in a straight, tight line and there was an unnaturally bright glitter in his eyes.

'They don't seem anxious to get any closer at the moment,' he observed.

Nevin nodded. 'I figure they'll be waitin' until they know how many men we have here before they try to rush us. After what happened at your place, we'll have to keep watch for men with torches. They may try to burn us out.'

'Yes, that remains a threat,' affirmed the other. His tone was grim.

By now, Nevin's eyes had become accustomed to the gloom and he was able to pick out several figures beginning a stealthy approach from one side, rushing forward in short runs, covered by the men at their back. They reached the corner of the corral and threw themselves down behind the wooden posts, hugging the ground, squeezing their bodies into the smallest possible volume. Nevin drew a bead on one of them, waited for the man to lift himself. A few moments later, the other pushed himself up on to hands and knees, presenting his back into the sights of Nevin's rifle. He waited for the barest fraction of a second before squeezing the trigger, feeling the gun buck against his wrist from the recoil. The man jerked as though struck in the middle of the back by a clenched fist and collapsed on to his face in the dust. Almost instantly, the dimness was split by the streaks of red flame from ready held guns. Vicious streaks of light speared out into the darkness, blossoming from the shadows. Nevin saw another man move, running forward, his head bent low. He dived for the cover of a trough which had been too heavy to move and Nevin squeezed off a shot as the other wriggled out of sight, thrusting himself along the ground with desperate heaves of his legs. The slugs kicked up dust behind him as he squirmed forward.

Lead from the rifles in the distance came reaching out for the house. The glass in the window beside Nevin crashed into the room as two bullets ploughed through it. A third slug hummed through the air and buried itself in the wall on the far side of the room. More bullets bit deeply into the outer walls. Nevin flinched in spite of the grip he had on himself, forcing calm into the thudding beat of his heart as it hammered against his ribs. He concentrated on snapping shots at the enemy, aiming at their muzzle flashes.

Finally, he realized that so long as the enemy remained on the edge of the cleared ground, they were merely wasting lead trying to hit them. Aiming for the house was a totally different matter to aiming for a man, moving from one shadow to another in the darkness, two hundred yards away.

'Hold your fire,' he called loudly, so that his voice would reach the men in the other rooms. 'We're just wastin' precious ammunition right now. Save your bullets for the rushes that'll be comin' soon, once they pluck up their courage to really attack.'

The firing slackened. Clayton's men, having surrounded the entire place, continued to fire at the ranch-house and the barn, but their bullets were causing no casualties, would not do so provided the defenders kept their heads down. The men did not relax their vigilance.

'Can you see anythin'?' Nevin asked tightly.

Dawney shook his head, moved back instinctively as a bullet smacked the frame of the window, sending a spear of wood flying into the room. It caught Nevin on the side of the face, gouging deeply into his flesh. Pulling it out with a sudden jerk, he felt the blood gush warmly down his cheek and on to his hand.

'They'll wait until it gets real dark before they try to rush us,' he said harshly. 'When they do, they'll probably come at us from all sides.'

'We'll fight 'em off,' Dawney said tightly. He checked his Colts, then thrust them back into their holsters. 'What has happened to Bob? You figure he's still all right?'

'I hope so,' echoed the other fervently. 'If he did manage to stop any of Clayton's bunch, and judgin' by their fire, I'd say that he hasn't got all of his men here, it's possible that he did. If so, he may be ridin' back right now to take these coyotes from the rear. That ought to throw enough confusion into their ranks to give us a chance to go out and finish 'em.'

The darkness grew more intense. As yet, there had been no sound apart from the gunfire outside, but suddenly, they heard Clayton's voice, calling from the rocky ground on the perimeter of the courtyard.

'You in there, Nevin?'

Ben grinned viciously. He moved his body slightly, called back: 'I'm here, Clayton. What's on your mind? Want to make a deal like you did with the Killearns?'

'No. I just don't see why we should be fightin' like this, killin' each other. I'll increase my offer for your place. Ten thousand dollars. You can't afford to turn that down. If you do, then we'll finish you completely, burn that ranch around your ears. I figure that if the men you hired to work for you knew just why they're bein' asked to risk their lives to protect you, they might change their minds a mite.'

'Somehow, I don't think so.' There was a grim tightness in Nevin's tone. 'We all know how much you can be trusted. The minute any of us show our faces out there, we'll be shot down.'

'If you're hopin' that your son will ride up to help you, then you're hopin' in vain, Nevin. He's finished. We cornered him back there in the hills, killed every man in the bunch.'

Nevin felt a cold twist of fear in his chest, but he forced it away at once. 'You're lyin', Clayton. Bob's still alive.'

'We'll see.' The other's voice faded into silence and a moment later, as though the man had realized that nothing would be gained by talking, the gunfire started up again. This time, it came from a little closer to the ranch and Nevin saw that while the other had been talking, his men had taken the opportunity to creep forward over the ground unnoticed, snaking forward on their bellies, making no sound in the dust.

Shots came whining in to the wall. Chips of splintered wood fell from the edge of the window. Jerking his Colts from their holsters, Nevin straightened to brave the flying lead as he caught sight of the sudden movement outside. A volley of shots crashed out from behind the running group of men in an attempt to force the defenders to keep their heads down. What Nevin saw caused him to yell a warning to Dawney. The two of them moved into the open windows, firing rapidly, the hammer of their guns adding to the thunder of the rifle barrage.

The spitting flames lit the night and the atmosphere thickened with blue gunsmoke. Orange flashes winked and spurted from all directions. But the intense and accurate revolver fire proved to be too much for the running gunmen. Those still on their feet paused, then turned and fled back the way they had come, bullets pursuing them, smashing into their unprotected backs, pitching them forward on to their faces in the dirt where they lay still, arms and legs outflung.

The thunder of the gunfire, carrying over the top of the hill, was heard as a faint crackle of sound by the small bunch of men spurring their mounts through the impeding timber which lay across their trail. Bob Nevin bent low in the saddle, urged his horse on at a punishing pace. He felt sorry for the animal, having to push it like this after the long day's trail, but there was no other alternative. The steady volleys which echoed from the distance were a sufficient indication that Clayton had joined forces with the small bunch of men which had succeeded in getting away from them earlier that day and they were now attacking the ranch. As yet there was no angry orange glow lighting the sky to show that the attackers had succeeded in starting a fire, but this danger was uppermost in Bob's mind as he kicked spurs into his horse's flanks.

By the time they came out of the trees, on to the trail that wound along the lee of the hill, the firing in the distance had settled down to a steady roll of sound. There was no need for caution as far as they were concerned. Clayton would have taken all of his men into the attack, leaving nobody to watch the trail. Having lost so many men that day, he could not afford to set guards to watch for anyone riding in on them from the rear, even though he would probably have considered it and would have liked to have done so.

Bob felt a sense of growing elation in him as he spurred towards the crest of the hill. This was the showdown. On the outcome of this gun battle depended who would rule this stretch of territory, the ranchers who had been there since the end of the war, or the mining company which meant to move in by force and hold the land the same way, bringing the old ways of violence with them, caring nothing for human life, destroying everything and everyone who dared to stand in their way.

From the top of the hill, among the small stand of trees, they were able to look down on the scene in the valley beneath them. Bob had reined up his mount, signalling to the rest of the men to do likewise. Nothing would be gained by riding down there and acting impulsively. This had to be thought out, to determine the best way to go about defeating Clayton. A quick glance was enough to tell him that the other had placed his men in a vast circle which entirely surrounded the ranch and outlying buildings, so that nobody there could get away to fetch help.

'How many men do you figure he's got left now?' asked Matt, sidling up to him quietly.

'Still too many for us to hope to beat him openly,' Bob replied. He turned his head to view the disposition of Clayton's force. Although he had surrounded the Circle Four ranch, there was one fundamental weakness there. His men were thin on the ground at every point. It would be relatively simple to smash a way through that circle of men.

'What are you thinkin', Bob?'

'I'm wonderin' if we can move in on the circle at this point, directly below us, and smash it, forcing Clayton to bring in his horns a little. That distraction should be sufficient to enable the others in the ranch and bunkhouse to break out and take them from the other side.'

Matt rubbed his chin. 'It might work at that,' he agreed. 'Clayton though must know by now that we're not far behind him.'

'He may not know how close. We made good time along the trail durin' the afternoon and evenin'.'

Bob drew his Colts, checked the cylinders, then returned them to their holsters. There was a grim tightness in him as he slid from the saddle, watching while the rest of the men did likewise. Motioning to the men to follow him quietly, he led the way through the ankle-deep grass which muffled their footfalls and then down towards the stretch of barren ground which fronted the ranch. Lead screeched perilously close to them as they slithered forward, some of it evidently coming from the house itself. Keeping low, they wormed themselves into a position for an attack. In front of them, the battle was on in earnest and one way or another, one side was doomed to extinction before it was finished and men were sure to die.

The crashing thunder of shots blended into a curious roll of sound that almost deafened them as they crouched down with drawn weapons, waiting for Bob's signal to open fire. It was possible to make out the dark shapes of the gunmen, crouched among the boulders, even when there were no orange muzzle flashes to give their positions away.

Their first volley took the gunmen completely by surprise. Engaged in shooting at the ranch house, they had their backs to the men crouched down behind them and half a dozen men died before they were aware of this fresh menace at the rear. The few who did manage to turn, squirming for fresh cover, immediately showed fight. Bob felt the lead lash through the air close to his head and spang off the rocks on all sides as the gunmen drew hasty aim, firing blindly into the darkness. But surprised and demoralised, the gunmen in front of Bob and his men went under and when the gunsmoke cleared, there were none of them still alive.

Clayton had evidently seen the new attack, knew instantly what it foreshadowed. He was shouting orders in the distance, warning the rest of his men, moving some of them across to deal with this attack against his flank. Sucking in a deep breath, Bob strained to make out the moving shadows on their right, swinging in on them as Clayton issued his commands. What happened next was remembered only as disconnected incidents whenever he came to look back on it afterwards.

Gunfire seemed to leap out at them from every direction.

Something scorched along his arm and he almost dropped his gun with the terrific pain of it. He triggered a quick shot at a man who loomed up out of the darkness, seeming to rise from under Bob's feet. The Colt in the other's hand was lining up inexorably on Bob's chest as he squeezed off a single shot that caught the other in the V of his throat, just below the chin and above the breastbone. For a second, the man remained on his feet, his face bearing a stupid expression of stunned amazement, lips hanging slackly open. Then all of his muscles seemed to lose their control, to come apart. His body flopped forward, arms clutching at Bob's legs in an attempt to stay upright.

Savagely, he kicked out at the other before the man's inert weight could bring him down to his knees. The dead body fell away and Bob stepped over it, firing continually at running shapes which loomed up out of the night and vanished just as tantalizingly.

Slowly, however, caught between the crossfire, the firing was beginning to diminish in volume. The attackers were being forced into the open, nearer and nearer to the ranch-house, where the defenders brought their accurate fire to bear with terrible results. Within ten minutes, the courtyard was littered with the dead bodies of Clayton's men who had been cut down in the open before they had any chance at all of finding cover. Confused, they ran in all directions, with Clayton himself bellowing hoarsely in the background, striving to give orders and rally them.

But the gunmen were too far gone to respond to his call. He had held them together, welded them into a single unit because of his savage ruthlessness and the fact that he seemed to have everything going his way. So long as they were called upon to attack a handful of homesteaders and burn them out of their place, they were quite happy, but when it came to facing determined men who seemed now to outnumber them, then it was a different matter. They no longer thought of any allegiance they owed to Clayton. He was just another man in the same predicament as they themselves. They began to scatter, to run for the cover of the hills, searching out their horses, ready to ride out over the hills and keep on riding. Fanning out and shooting rapidly as they ran, they moved back to their mounts.

Sizing up the situation, Bob ordered his men to go after them, to hunt them down before they could reach their mounts and ride out. Running forward, Bob sought out Clayton. At first, he could see no sign of the other although he knew roughly where he was hidden from the sound of his voice. Then he saw the dark shadow that moved back into the grass, bending low to present a more difficult target and to escape being seen.

Treading softly, Bob went after the other, struggling forward up the steep slope. Clayton was almost at the top when he suddenly turned, stared behind him and saw Bob close on his heels.

'So it's you, Nevin,' he snarled. 'I figured that we would have to meet face to face sometime. Everythin' was goin' right for me until you rode in.'

'Just hold it right there,' Bob said warningly. 'I'm takin' you in for trial. I reckon there are plenty of charges I can make against you, and it won't be Judge Mender tryin' you this time. We'll get somebody from Dallas and they can try you, the judge and that crooked sheriff you've got in town all together.'

Clayton shook his head slowly. 'You won't take me in, Nevin. But I'll make sure that I take you with me.' As he spoke his hand flashed down for the gun at his waist. His fingers were a blur of speed. They had closed over the butt of the gun were in the act of jerking it from leather when the gun in Bob Nevin's hand spoke flame and smoke The slug took the other high up in the chest, jerking him fully upright. The gun in his hand tilted downward, hung for a moment and then dropped into the grass. Somehow, Clayton managed to lift his head. The eyes that stared across at Bob were filled with a feral hatred that surpassed anything Nevin had seen before.

Then they were glazing over rapidly. The man swayed drunkenly as he strove with all of his rapidly failing strength to stay on his feet, to remain upright. For a moment longer, he managed to do so. Then his lips parted, a long, bubbling sigh came out of them and he collapsed on to his knees one hand fluttering up to his torn chest. He tried to say something as he knelt there swaying from side to side but only a low moan came through his teeth before he crashed forward and lay still.

Bob went forward, turned the other over with his toe, saw the limp manner in which he flopped back, then turned away and walked back in the direction of the ranch. The last few shots died away into an all-pervading stillness that seemed to hurt the ears as much as the racketing din which had preceded it. With the fighting over, the men came forward from cover while others came out of the house and bunkhouse.

'It's finished,' said Ben Nevin quietly. He thrust the hot Colt back into its holster, surveyed the scene of carnage in front of the house. 'What happened to Clayton? Did he get away?'

'He didn't get far,' Bob said thinly. 'He's dead, up there on the side of the hill. He came because he was so confident that he would win, and now he's dead, because he couldn't conceive the possibility of failure.'

'And those men who rode with him?'

'They're gone. They'll take the trail over the hill and keep riding. He was the only thing which held them here. With him dead, they're broken and scattered. They'll go back to jumpin' from one trail to another, tryin' their damnedest to stay ahead of the law.'

'Tomorrow we'll ride into town and pick up that crooked sheriff if he's still around, clap him in jail and try him for bein' in cahoots with Clayton. The same goes for Mender.'

Bob wiped the smoke and dust from his face, then made his way slowly to the house, into the small front parlour. There was splintered glass all over the floor and bullet holes in the walls. June Dawney was there with a brush, trying to clear up some of the mess. She pushed a stray curl from her eyes as he entered, gave a glad little cry and ran into his arms.

'We heard Clayton say that you had been killed with all of the others,' she said wonderingly.

'I reckon he was hopin' that you might give in if you heard that.' He tightened his arms around her waist. 'Now we can all start and build something better here. Once we get word through to Dallas, I reckon we'll hear no more about the mining company's claims to this land.'

June Dawney nodded. He eyes were shining but she said nothing. Bending, Bob kissed her gently on the lips, then released her as the rest of the men came in. Outside, the yellow moon lifted above the hill, flooded the courtyard with its pale light.

—